MW00592292

 **THE
FIRST STREET CHURCH ROMANCES
BOOK ONE**

Love's Prayer

MELISSA STORM

LOVE'S PRAYER Copyright © 2016 Partridge & Pear Press. All rights reserved. You may not use, reproduce or transmit in any manner, any part of this book without written permission, except in the case of brief quotations used in critical articles and reviews, or in accordance with federal Fair Use laws.

ISBN 10: 1942771347
ISBN 13: 9781942771340

Editor:
Stevie Mikayne

Cover and Interior Design:
Mallory Rock

Proofreader:
Falcon Storm

PO Box 72
Brighton, MI 48116

Love's Prayer is a work of fiction. Names, characters, places and incidents are products of the author's imagination, or the author has used them fictitiously.

* * *

To all the people who face the darkness of depression but still manage to find their smiles in the end.

To Falcon.

FREE GIFT

Thank you for picking up your copy of *Love's Prayer*. I so hope you love it! As a thank you, I'd like to offer you a free gift. That's right, I've written a short story that's available exclusively to my newsletter subscribers. You'll receive the free story by email as soon as you sign up at www.MelStorm.com/Newsletter. I hope you'll enjoy both stories. Happy reading!

Melissa

Chapter 1

Ben Davis had once believed in God. He had once believed in miracles, fate, divine intervention, and all the similar lies people told themselves to get through the day. Perhaps if he still believed, he wouldn't find himself so tempted to stay in bed all day, to never get up—not even to eat—and to eventually die a slow, private death in the only place that still offered him any comfort at all.

On this day, a Thursday, he spent longer than usual blinking up at the ceiling and wondering if he should just end it all with a swift bullet to the brain. After all, that's what his older brother Stephen had done roughly five years ago. He'd wandered off into the town square and shot himself clean in the face for all of Sweet Grove to see. People were still talking about it to this day, and those who didn't speak of it were most definitely thinking of it.

Like his mother. She waded through the memories, attempting to silence them with the bottle. But even though the liquor often ran out, her grief remained endless, unquenchable.

Ben wasn't saddened by the loss of his brother. Even though he sometimes felt as if he should be. No, he was angry—his rage another unquenchable commodity in the Davis household. Stephen had selfishly chosen to end it all. He'd hurled his issues straight at Ben who, ever since that day, had been tasked with paying the mortgage, tending to their mother who had spiraled down the dark path of addiction, and without an outlet to enjoy any of the things he had spent years working toward and hoping for.

He'd turned down his full-ride scholarship to college because he needed to take care of things here in Sweet Grove—things that only got worse the more his mother was left to grapple with her grief. Recovery remained a summit she just couldn't reach, no matter how hard she climbed. So he'd turned the university down year after year, and eventually the admissions board had just stopped asking.

Which left him here today, staring up at the

popcorn ceiling above his twin-sized bed, no longer bothering to wonder if life could ever be any different. At 6:12, he placed one foot after another onto the shaggy carpet below and went to clean up for work. At 6:25, he was out the door with a piece of half-cooked toast in one hand and a banana in the other. He had five minutes to make the short walk from the quaint— and "quaint" was putting it kindly—home he shared with his mother to the local market where he worked as a bagger and delivery boy. Yes, even his job title suggested a more temporary arrangement, a job better suited to a boy than the man he had become—although only just barely. And he still worked here.

"Good morning!" sang his boss Maisie Bryant as he tromped through the sliding glass doors. Each morning she arranged a fresh display of local produce and other seasonal specialties right at the front of the shop. As always, she took great pride in her work.

Ben hated that his boss was only a couple years older than him. Maisie had managed to escape town long enough to earn a degree before coming back to run her family's grocery store. While he didn't know the exact numbers, he could bet that the youngest Bryant child made at least triple what he did for the same day's work. But that was life for you—or at least for Ben. Never fair, not in the least.

"Don't I get a hello?" Maisie teased him as always. Some days he liked her chipper demeanor. This was not one of those days.

"Hi," he mumbled. "I'm going to go check the stock. See you in a bit."

"Wait," she called before he could manage to make his escape. "I'll handle the stock. The staff over at Maple's called, and they need a delivery first thing. Think you can handle that? The purchase order is on the clock desk."

"Yeah, I got it."

Ben hurried to put the order together and load up the designated Sweet Grove Market truck. A smiling red apple beamed from the side of the cargo hold. He hated that thing, but he did like having the opportunity to drive around a little, let the wind wash over him as he rolled about town. It sure beat walking everywhere, and since it offered his only opportunity to get behind the wheel, he relished every chance he got. Occasionally, Maisie would let him borrow the truck to head into the next town over and lose himself in the sea of unfamiliar faces.

He'd once loved living in the type of place where everyone knew everyone and everyone looked out for everyone, but he hated how people who had once been his friends had begun to pity him. Ever since Stephen's death, they couldn't even look at him without betraying that sadness. Ben had become a reminder of how fragile life could be, of how everything could go to hell in the briefest of moments. And though their words were kind and their smiles were omnipresent, Ben knew better. He knew that he'd become a burden to them all, that his presence brought them sorrow.

At first he'd tried to redirect them, to speak of something—anything—else, but after a while he just grew tired. It was easier to avoid them than to constantly have to apologize for the blight his terrible, selfish brother had brought onto their town. He'd have left if he could. Rather by vehicle or bullet, it didn't matter.

But his mother needed him. And as small and insignificant as it seemed, so did Maisie.

So he remained, day after day.

And so began another dark morning for Ben Davis.

Summer Smith arrived in Sweet Grove right around that awkward time of day when the sun was starting to set and ended up in her eyes no matter how hard she tried to look away. She loved sunshine, which is why she'd jumped at the chance to attend college in California, but now those four years had reached their conclusion and had left Summer more confused than ever about her future.

Thank goodness her Auntie Iris needed her to run the Morning Glory shop for the season. She was jetting off on some fancy cruise she'd been saving up for half her adult life. True, that didn't speak well of the money to be earned operating a small town florist's, but then again, Summer had never been much taken with flowers anyhow.

The problem remained that she'd never really been much taken with anything in life. And now that she'd reached that pivotal stage of needing to pick a career and finally set down roots, she was hopelessly lost. Two months, one week, and three days—that's how much time she had to figure it out. At that point, Auntie Iris would return from her sail around the world and be ready to take back her shop and home. So for the next two months and some-odd days, Summer would be living a borrowed life. Luckily, she'd always liked her Aunt Iris.

The old spinster greeted her at the door wearing a brightly colored blouse with leaf fronds printed along the neckline, and with freshly dyed hair that still smelled of chemicals. "Oh, there's my Sunny Summer!" she cooed.

Summer laughed as her aunt hopped up and down, still holding her tight. The hug probably could have lasted for days if a loud screeching hadn't erupted from deep within the small ranch house.

Iris let go of her niece and breezed through the doorway, dragging the smaller of Summer's suitcases behind her. "Oh, enough, Sunny Sunshine!" she called, leaving Summer to wonder if her aunt affixed *Sunny* to the start of everyone's name these days.

The shrieking continued, growing louder as they made their way back toward the living room. There, in the far corner beside the small stone fireplace, sat a large iron cage with a colorful blur of feathers which screamed its lungs out.

Iris rushed over and unlatched the cage, then drew out the little bird on a delicately poised finger. "Now that's not how you make a good first impression. Is it, Sunny?"

The bird ruffled its feathers like a little marigold flower then shook itself out.

Iris laughed. "Much better. Now meet Summer." She puckered her lips and blew a stream of air at the little bird, who made a happy bubble-like noise. Iris then offered the parrot to Summer who took a giant leap back.

"I-I just… You didn't say anything about a bird!"

"Oh, Sunny won't be any bother. Besides, you'll be grateful for the company once you're settled in and looking for a bit of fun."

"I tend to prefer the company of humans."

"Sunny is the human-est bird you will ever meet. Aren't you, my baby?" She placed the little Conure on her shoulder and he immediately burrowed below the neckline of her blouse and stuck his head back up through the hole, making Iris look like a strange two-headed monster. Summer had to admit that Sunny *was* cute. Maybe she and the bird could come to some kind of agreement during their months together.

Iris—bird in tow—showed Summer around the house, pointing out which plants needed to be watered when and taking extra care when it came to describing the needs of her little feathered friend.

"Is that it?" Summer asked when the two had settled onto the loveseat following the grand tour.

"Pretty much. What else do you need to know?"

"How to run the shop, for one. Also, what am I going to do with myself to keep busy during the nights?"

"I've written everything down in a big binder and left it for you near the cash register. Everything in the shop is clearly marked as well. You'll use the key with the daisy head to open up shop. Hours are eight to three. And as for how you'll keep busy…" Her eyes flashed as she bit back a Cheshire cat-sized smile. "Life in a small town is never boring. You'll see."

"But, Auntie Iris, aren't you worried I'll mess things up with the shop?"

Iris waved a hand dismissively. "You'll figure things out."

Summer wasn't sure whether her aunt was talking about running the shop or about life in general. Either way, Summer sure hoped she was right.

Chapter 2

After work that Thursday, Ben headed over to the one place in town where he still felt like himself—or at least the self he had been prior to that fatal gunshot that had ripped his life clean to shreds.

"Good evening, Ben. I was wondering if we'd see you again this week," said the librarian Sally Scott with a smile as she glanced up from the big circular desk where she sat reading a thick paperback novel.

"Would've been here all day every day if I could, but this week has been… rough." He sighed, thinking back to his mother's blackout on Tuesday and how he'd had to watch her to make sure she continued to breathe as she coughed, choked, and vomited through the night.

"Well, I'm glad you made it in today." Sally smiled again and resumed her reading. Ben liked that she never asked too much nor did she constantly apologize about what had happened with Stephen. When they talked, they exchanged pleasantries like this most recent exchange, or they discussed intellectual things—history, science, academia. All the topics that brought Ben back to life at the end of a hard day.

Sally had never once asked him why he preferred to spend hours in the stacks rather than simply checking out the books to take home. She never pried, never pressed, and in a way that absence of curiosity made her his best friend in all of Sweet Grove. Sad that his criteria for friendship was someone who respected him well enough to leave him be.

Today he planned to catch up on Tsarist Russia. He liked finding out how the cartoonish antics of their parade of despots somehow eventually led the over-drinked, under-heated country to twentieth-century super power-dom. It somehow gave him hope that greatness could still spring from his life as well. A small hope, but still hope nonetheless.

He licked his forefinger and turned to the section on Ivan the Terrible, one of the cruelest yet most productive figures in all of the world's history. But the story of how he beat his daughter-in-law until she miscarried and then killed his own son when he tried to intervene was too much after the week he'd had. How could the *ancient* history of a far-off land still feel so new, so personal?

Ivan had destroyed so many things during his reign and ultimately had left his mentally incompetent son Feodor as heir to the Russian throne. Was that because anyone with the strength to challenge Ivan's terribleness ended up dead at his feet? And did that make Ben himself like poor, disabled Feodor—too stupid and too kind to stand up for himself?

Oh, it certainly felt that way as he continued to bring his mother the liquor she requested and to clean up after her once the liquid drug had taken its toll. He'd not only put his own pursuit of greatness on hold, he'd completely disbanded it. All so he could stay at home and help his mother destroy herself with her unwillingness to address the grief they both struggled with dayin and dayout.

Did that mean he was to blame for what his mother had become? That she may be better off without having him around as an enabler? Still there was no money, which meant the only way out would be by the same road his brother had taken—the one that led straight to hell.

But this was hell already, wasn't it? Here he sat reading about the sadistic history of a country that wasn't even his own to somehow make himself feel better about *his* life. How far he'd fallen.

Ben took a deep breath and eased the book shut. Not even the library could offer comfort today. Hopefully a new day and a new topic of research could work to improve his mood, but what if they didn't? What if he no longer had a single place to which he belonged? What then?

"Leaving so soon?" Sally asked, this time with a frown.

"I'm not well," he said, speaking of his heart more than anything.

"Oh, well. Feel better!" She waved good-bye and then disappeared down a long row of books.

If only it were that easy, he thought, kicking at the pebbles that littered the sidewalk as he headed toward the house he shared with his mother. Would she be sober when he arrived? The fact that it no longer even mattered startled him once more. Only twenty-four and already his life had reached its natural end. Would it really be so wrong if he helped speed things up a bit? After all, that's what his brother had done. And more and more that seemed like the best thing for Ben as well.

Tomorrow was a new day. But would it wind up being his last? He couldn't say for certain.

The next morning, Summer awoke early to drive her aunt to the airport. After a quick good-bye, she returned to Sweet Grove to open up shop for the day. Finding the binder with the instructions her aunt had left out for her had been the easy part. Following them, though? The level of detail made her head hurt.

And apparently she was expected to bring Sunny Sunshine to the store each morning to help greet customers—transported in his travel cage. Summer groaned. Why couldn't Aunt Iris have warned her about that ahead of time? As it was, she still couldn't be sure whether she could so much as touch the tiny bird without receiving a mean nip in the process.

Well, that would be tomorrow's problem. Today had already presented enough to keep her busy until closing time rolled around. Like for instance, where and what was the raffia? And how was she supposed to know the difference between an aster and a daisy? Would she actually be expected to prep her own arrangements to sell to customers?

She wished her aunt would have taken more care in showing her the ropes before jetting off on her dream cruise. Sure, the instructions she had left were ridiculously detailed—practically a novel-sized tome—but Summer had always learned best through talking with others as she tried her own hand at new skills.

Maybe if she spoke the words aloud as she read?

"Always keep the cooler between thirty-four and thirty-six degrees. Otherwise the petals will brown. The controls are around the..." Summer trailed off when the tiny bell over the door jingled to announce a customer.

A sporty woman not much older than Summer walked swiftly into the space and took a deep breath in. She let out a slow exhale, her lips puckered but also smiling. Fixing her eyes on Summer, she said, "Ahh, you must be this Sunny Summer I've heard so much about. Elise Nelson. How you doing?"

"Yup, I'm Summer. Umm, just Summer, please. Nice to meet you." Summer shot out from behind the cashier's desk and offered her hand to the visitor. "My aunt must have told you all about me, huh?"

Elise shook her head and laughed. "Me and everyone else in town. Don't tell her I told you this, but Iris is kind of known as the town gossip. Hey, where's Sunny Sunshine? Is he taking the day off?"

"Oh, just for today so I can find my bearings before having to worry about yet another thing. To be honest, he kind of scares me."

"Oh, no. Sunny wouldn't hurt a fly. You'll see. Speaking of flying, I need to zoom out of here pretty quick. I just came to collect a bouquet for a sick friend of mine before visiting her in the hospital. I'm sorry I can't talk more. If you're half as wonderful as your aunt claims, then I just know you'll feel right at home in no time."

Elise spoke quickly but enunciated her words well. Unfortunately, Summer wasn't sure what she needed to do to fill the order.

Seeing her struggle, Elise piped up. "I placed the order yesterday morning and Iris said she'd set it aside. It's probably under my friend's name. Kristina Rose?"

"Thanks. Have I mentioned I'm totally out of my element here?" Summer jogged back to the cooler, and sure enough a cute and playful arrangement of daisies—or were they asters?—sat waiting for her. She scooped them up and placed them on the counter next to the cash register.

A huge smile broke out on Elise's pretty face. "Daisies. Kristina's favorite. These will really brighten her day. The poor thing just found out... *Hmm,* I suppose I shouldn't gossip. You'll know everything about everyone in Sweet Grove soon enough."

"I have no idea what to charge you for these," Summer admitted. "I haven't gotten to that part of

Aunt Iris's magnum opus yet." She held up the overstuffed binder and grimaced, pretending it was too heavy to lift.

"That's Iris for you all right. Look behind you." She pointed just over Summer's head. "I believe this is a medium wild flower bouquet, so it's twelve ninety-five."

Summer did a face palm. Literally hit herself in the forehead to show her embarrassment. How obvious had that answer been?

Elise chuckled and handed her a twenty, and thankfully Summer had no difficulties working the register. The many years of experience she'd garnered working at this or that fast food place while growing up proved useful.

"Will I see you this weekend in church?" Elise asked, accepting her change. "You're a little older than the others, but the youth group is having a special concert and I'd love to see you there and introduce you around. Oh, I'm the youth pastor, by the way. Did I mention that? Hey, if Kristina Rose is feeling better by then, you can meet her, too."

Summer hesitated. She'd been to church before, but had purposefully avoided it ever since moving out on her own. Life was hard enough without feeling judged at every turn, but at the same time, Elise

Nelson was kind, friendly, funny, and just the type of woman Summer normally found herself making fast friends with.

The youth pastor sensed her hesitation and waved her hand in front of her face as if batting at an invisible mosquito. "I didn't mean to put you on the spot there. Just know that you are always welcome. You'll find that everyone in this town is real nice, and I'm sure they'll each be stopping by soon enough to say their hellos. I'll come back around later too, but—man—I'm getting late. Thank you, and bye!"

Chapter 3

Ben looked out his bedroom window at the decaying yellow grass that made up his front lawn—if it still even deserved to be called a lawn. The yard had once been his mother's pride and joy. She'd planted all kinds of perennials along the brick house front and had gone out twice a day to water the grass. But the only plants that were thriving now were weeds that had long since choked out the far more beautiful blooms.

Weeds.

Ben's life had also been choked out by weeds. His mother's drinking was a weed. His brother's death was a weed. And the weed with the longest, deepest roots was undoubtedly the dream he had once pictured for himself. No longer did it bring him joy. Now every time he thought of the life he had once envisioned, he felt a deep sense of emptiness.

And without a life he wanted, what was the point of continuing to exist? Because that's all he was doing anymore—not living, *existing*. He stayed for Maisie, who could easily replace him at the store if it came right down to it, and he stayed for his mother. But she wasn't living either. If he were to leave, she'd either continue to drink herself into a daily oblivion or, finally, the grave. And frankly, neither option felt so much worse than the other.

Leaving to go elsewhere would, of course, be impossible. There was no money, and he'd never be able to escape the guilt if he abandoned his mother to face her demons alone. The only way out would be by his own hand—an option that seemed increasingly plausible these days.

Would dying hurt? And would hurting actually be such a bad thing? The days on which he felt sorrow, guilt, remorse, were a welcome change from the general numbness. But he wouldn't shoot himself like Stephen had, and none of the buildings in town were tall enough to jump from. Otherwise that seemed like a good, swift way to go.

He could tie himself to the train tracks that crisscrossed the town. It would have a certain poetry to it, given his love of history and his desire to shuttle himself from this world by any means necessary.

But death by train would simply take too long. This wasn't the big city with reliable schedules and a train every thirty minutes like clockwork. He'd need to wait, and waiting could make him lose his nerve. If he was going to do this thing, he needed to do it right. That way he could be proud of himself in his final moments. Achieve some small victory before he consigned himself to the history books.

No one would tell great tales of Ben Davis, though.

He'd get a single obituary cobbled together—by Maisie probably—and then the town would move on without him. It would be easy since he hadn't been much more than a shadow for years—a wisp of what he could have been, hanging on to that last thread of hope that continued to fray until there was simply nothing left to hold onto.

Hanging.

Yes, that would do it. He could pick up a rope from the store's tiny hardware section tomorrow. Come home, and…

Would tomorrow be too soon? Didn't he need a bit more time to plan?

Stephen had meticulously planned his suicide down to the letter. Yes, he had planned to make a public spectacle of himself and a mockery of his family. *That's* what he had wanted. Ben didn't want that. If he could find a way to avoid having anyone discover his dead body, then he would. But all bodies turned up eventually, didn't they? He couldn't control whatever happened after, but he *could* control his own actions leading up to the moment.

Today he would make his peace. Tomorrow he would put in an honest day's work, continue to plan, figure out the best way to perfect his final living act. Maybe tomorrow would be the day, or maybe he would need more time. Funny how he needed more time to figure out how to effectively end time, or at least his time on Earth.

Still… One way or another, he'd have his peace and he'd have it soon.

Ben padded out into the living room where his mother lay sprawled across the sofa, watching the daytime news. He hated days like this, but Maisie insisted that he take at least one shift off per week to relax and enjoy himself. What would she think when she found out that he'd spent his forced day off like this? He would never know, would he?

"Mom," he said, stepping in front of the TV. "Do you ever think about what happens to us when we die?"

She sat up a little straighter, took a swig of whisky and swallowed it down. "I don't need to think. I know. Your brother is in Heaven watching over us."

Ben bit back a laugh. If there was a Heaven, his brother surely wasn't in it. And if he were some kind of guardian angel for their family, he'd have long since been fired for poor job performance. "Does that make you feel better? Thinking about Stephen in Heaven?"

"He's an angel now, and angels don't feel sad," she said without moving her gaze from the television.

Ben watched her as she became reabsorbed in the news. He suspected she might have a crush on the male anchor for how much she fixated whenever he appeared on screen.

Her mouth hung open, slightly ajar, and she snorted when they switched to a sports story. "You're still here?" she asked, turning to discover that Ben had in fact stayed close by.

Will these be our final moments together? Our final words?

Just in case, he said, "I love you, Mom."

"You, too." The short sports report ended, and the screen was once again filled with the smile of Susan's favorite anchor. She smiled back at him, and for a moment she seemed genuinely happy.

Well, what had he expected from her? She'd formed coherent sentences and returned his declaration of love. That was a lot better than this could have gone.

Still, he felt unsatisfied as he returned to the solitude of his dingy childhood bedroom.

He needed to talk to someone in the wake of this enormous decision, and since his mother was otherwise engaged, that left someone Ben hadn't spoken with— or even believed in—in a very long time.

God.

And so Ben dropped to his knees and prayed.

"God, Jesus, whoever you are. If what they say about you is true, then you've been where I am. You stared death down and didn't back away. And they praise you for it. But the difference, I think, is you didn't want to die. *I do.* I want to die so bad, it actually gives me a purpose in life." He laughed bitterly and choked back a sob.

"I don't know whether it's better that you don't exist or that you do exist but chose to give me this terrible life. I didn't deserve this, you know. Then again, maybe you made a mistake and I was supposed to have another life, a better one. But if you can make such a giant mistake, then who are you even, and why do people worship you? No, if you're real then you're oblivious, evil or just a jerk. Not somebody I'd want to know.

"But I'm desperate here, and that's why I'm calling on you. I…" A sob filled his chest, but he forced it back. "I need help. Please? If there's a way to repair my life, please do it soon. If not, I'll see you on the other side, provided you're real and there even is another side. I don't know. It doesn't matter. I just want—"

The doorbell gonged, breaking him away from his prayer.

"*Ben!*" his mother called from the couch. "*Door!*"

"I'm coming," he called, stumbling to his feet and wiping away the tears that had begun to spill across his cheeks.

On the other side of the door, a large arrangement of flowers sat waiting on the stoop. Puzzled, Ben reached for the card.

It read: *With all my love, your secret admirer.*

No, these definitely weren't for him or for his mother. There had been some kind of mistake. What timing!

He looked around for the delivery person, only to see a small blue sedan turning off his street and back into the traffic of the larger road.

Well, shoot.

At least returning the flowers would give him a reason to leave the house. It's not as if he had anything more to say or do today. No, all that would come later.

Summer raced from one floral arrangement to the next. Suddenly, Morning Glory's was flooded with rush orders and she was having a hard time keeping up. Her aunt hadn't told her what to do if she ran out of stock before the following week's delivery, and now she wondered if it would really be so wrong to prepare red roses or yellow daffodils for the out-of-town funeral so many residents were flocking to.

She frantically flipped through the giant binder to find the name and number for the supplier. Maybe they could rush out some lilies to help meet demand. Seriously, who knew the flower business was so tough!

The bell over the door jingled, and Summer tried not to frown as she looked up to see which customer she'd be disappointing this time. A giant bouquet of roses floated into the shop. Behind them, a good-looking but obviously upset young man about her age. His hair was blondish, his skin tanned, and his green eyes would have been irresistibly gorgeous had there been any light in them.

Oh, no. What have I messed up now?

Summer smiled at her customer, but he did not return the gesture.

"I think I got these by mistake, so I'm just bringing them back." His low baritone lacked affectation, despite the adorable Texas drawl.

"Oh, I'm so sorry!"

"It's fine. I wasn't doing anything important anyway. Have a good day." He stuck his hands in his pockets and turned to leave, but Summer shot out from behind the counter and blocked his path.

"Wait, don't go!"

"I'm sorry, but I have something I need to do…" It seemed like he wanted to say more, but he just stood there staring at her. His face twisted in a scowl.

"Look, I know I don't know you and you don't know me, and I totally believe that I made a mistake and that those flowers were meant for someone else. Honestly, I'm so sure of it, I don't even need to check. But I'm kind of dying here trying to keep up with all these orders, and—oh!—I really shouldn't say it like that. Not when someone actually died. Did you know Rebecca James? Everyone is putting in orders for her funeral even though it's out of town, and I don't have enough flowers, and I can't even properly deliver the ones I do have, and I'm just so overwhelmed, and—and—and…"

Oh, please don't cry! Please don't cry! Summer fanned herself in a desperate attempt to regain her cool.

"Ben."

"What?" she croaked, just on the edge of a full-out bawl.

"I'm Ben. How can I help?"

"Oh, thank you, thank you, thank you! You know that song by Sheryl Crow? You're my favorite mistake? I'm sorry I sent you that order by mistake, but—boy—am I glad I did! It's like fate brought you here to help me out. Because I swear, I'm about to lose it, and, and…" The tears threatened again and Ben reluctantly patted her on the shoulder.

"No problem. I'll stay for a little bit and pitch in. Okay?"

"Okay," she sniffed. "By the way, I'm Summer. And you, Ben, are my new best friend."She reached her arms around him and gave him a tight, enthusiastic hug.

He stiffened in her arms, but she didn't care. Having another real live person here to help out made all the difference in the world right then.

"What can I do to help?" he asked, pulling away and pacing toward the cooler. It already looked like he knew what he was doing more than she did.

Summer chewed her lower lip as she thought, then said, "Let's figure out where those roses you brought in were supposed to go, and then I need to figure out how to get more lilies in here so I can start filling some of these orders."

She shuffled through the huge stack of note paper at the cashier's desk, searching for the details on the arrangement Ben had just returned. "*Huh*, that's weird."

"What?" He came around the counter to look over her shoulder.

"Seventeen-oh-one May Lane," she said, pointing to the place on the page where she had scribbled the order details. "I could have sworn that's where I dropped them off. Is that your neighbor or something?"

"No, that *is* my address."

"Oh, shoot. Then I must have taken the order down wrong. With all my love, your secret admirer," she read aloud, then gave Ben a knowing smile. "Are you *sure* you don't have a secret admirer?"

"I don't think I've ever been so sure of something in my entire life," he quipped and finally—*finally!*—

graced Summer with a smile of his own. It helped, but not enough to make her feel better about making such an awful mistake.

"I'm really not cut out for this," she said with a sigh. "Luckily, it's only for a couple months while my Aunt Iris is away on her cruise."

"Well, let's make the most of the time we have. That's all any of us can do, right?"

She looked up at him and his eyes locked on hers as if he were searching for some kind of answer—but not one she had.

"Sure, I guess. Okay, let's do this." She tossed the order slips back into the drawer and then picked up the binder. "Are you sure you don't mind staying to help for a while? I thought you said you had something important to do?"

"It can wait," he said, fingering the petals on one of the roses in the arrangement that still sat nearby. "It can wait."

Chapter 4

Something had begun to crack light into Ben's dark heart, and her name was Summer Smith. He'd stayed on for about an hour to help her sort out orders, and then had borrowed her car to go pick up some new arrangements on rush order. There had been no shortage of hugs and thank yous and truly genuine smiles that afternoon, either.

By the time Ben returned home for the day, he found that even he wore a smile on his normally placid face. Was he really so simple? Was this all it took to give his life meaning again—a pretty girl and a few kind words?

It seemed ridiculous that all his problems could be solved so easily, and yet...

He didn't know why he had stayed to help in the first place. Or, for that matter, why he'd even ventured to return the wrongly delivered flowers. Perhaps it all came down to the fact that Ben had always put others before himself. Normally that meant simply doing a good job at any tasks assigned to him, being pleasant more or less, and staying out of people's way. But Summer was different. She actually needed him—and that felt great.

Somehow helping her run Morning Glory's for that afternoon had become the most important thing he'd done in recent memory, which was really quite pathetic. Still... maybe it was a start to finding his way back to happiness in life.

Maybe things weren't all bad, after all. Maybe there might be a reason to stay.

Of course, the most pressing question was whether he had the girl to thank or the situation. Would helping anyone have put him into such good spirits, or was this new feeling of warmth because he had helped *her* specifically?

Going about his morning the following day, he kept turning this question over in his mind. While he replenished the shelves in aisle three with fresh stock, Ben pictured her smile. As he reviewed the orders that had come in from assorted local businesses, he felt as if her arms had wrapped around him in thanks once again. And he smiled, which is not something he had done much of these past few years. But today he just couldn't help himself. It felt good to have lightness in his heart once again. He only hoped he could hold on to it for long enough to make an actual, lasting difference in his life.

Ben sighed as he realized that it probably wouldn't. As time went on, the memory of that afternoon would fade. The only way to keep this newfound hope alive would be to replenish it with more time in Summer's company. And how could he just show up at her shop unannounced and volunteer his services once again? He didn't want to insult her by implying she couldn't keep things running without his help, and the thought of asking her on a date made his stomach turn.

What if she said no? He'd rather think fondly of her and wonder *what if* than find himself facing a real-life rejection. And somehow he couldn't see things ending in his favor, no matter how hard he tried. No. It would definitely be best to savor his memories while they lasted and see how he felt once they no longer cheered him. Would he find a new reason to feel happy, or was this his last grab at bliss? His last grab, and already he had loosened his fingers and let it float away.

This was why Ben constantly found himself stuck in a dark hole, because he was too afraid to climb out and face the sunshine, to let summer reign.

And then, suddenly, there she was, live and in the flesh… and standing just a half a store's length away, chatting with Maisie as the two looked over a fresh flower delivery.

Summer frowned and shook her head, and Maisie placed a conciliatory hand on her shoulder. *Another mistake?* Probably, but Maisie was too good-natured to make much of it. She would sell whatever Summer had brought, and she would do so happily. Ben envied her in that way, that Maisie always made the best of everything. But then again, she'd been born into the wealthiest family in town and had everything handed to her along the way. Ben liked to believe he would share her sunny outlook had he been blessed with the same circumstances.

Noticing him then, Summer smiled and gave an enthusiastic wave.

Oh, crap. Had he been staring this whole time? Ben nodded curtly and then retreated down the aisle pretending he had something important to do.

Coward! He'd spent all of last night and this morning pining away for her, and when she actually showed up he couldn't run away fast enough. *See, Ben. This is why you don't deserve nice things.* His inner critic continued to taunt him as he fled for the back of the store. Just as quickly as hope had filled his heart, it circled the drain, and disappeared.

Had Summer really just screwed up another order? Well, at least Maisie was being nice about it. She smiled at Summer while placing the baskets and vases Summer had just delivered into a beautiful display at the front of her store.

Maisie shook Summer offer whenever she tried to apologize. "Sure, it's not what I ordered, but there's no denying these flowers are gorgeous. My customers are going to grab these up lickety split, and before you know it, I'll be placing a whole new order from Morning Glory's."

"Are you sure?" Summer wondered if she was ever going to get things right—or at least get them right before the end of her stay in Sweet Grove.

"Oh, honey, you're fine! Stop worrying so much. Just slowdown, relax, take some time to smell the roses. Oh, look! Here are some now." Maisie laughed as she pushed a bouquet of yellow roses toward Summer's nose.

Summer laughed too as she leaned in and took a good, long whiff of the fragrant petals."Well, I can already tell I'm going to like you. I'm just sorry I didn't get the order right. Next time though…"

"Oh, no, no, no you don't. What did I just say about the roses? Seems to me you're just trying too hard, and that's causing you to get all sorts of flustered. I bet you haven't even taken the time to show yourself around Sweet Grove. Am I right?" Maisie crossed her arms over her chest as she waited for Summer's response.

Summer shrugged. "Is it that obvious that I'm new around here?"

"This is a small town, and everybody knows *everybody*. Besides, your Aunt Iris is a good friend of mine. I've been hearing about her cruise for… Must be years now. I swear, the very same day I took over the market, your Aunt Iris was here delivering flowers and introducing me to Sunny Sunshine while telling me all about the trip she had planned, just as soon as she could afford to take it. I'm so happy for her, by the way."

Summer chuckled. "Yes, that's my Aunt Iris for you. She always has a smile on her face and a story to tell. Well, almost always. When I got here, all she wanted to do was show me how to take care of Sunny Sunshine and tell me all about life in Sweet Grove. Actually, she *did* mention you. She said—"

Maisie interrupted with a long drawn out sigh. "Why does that not surprise me?"

Then a bright smile returned to her face as she said, "Iris does have a certain reputation for gossip, but she means no harm. In a way, she's Sweet Grove's alternative to having a local newspaper. With her around, we've just never needed one. You want to know what's going on, you ask Iris. Speaking of, will you be taking over that role too while she's away?"

"Well, I haven't met too many people yet, so I wouldn't know what to gossip about. But I'd certainly be happy to try. What do I need to know? Maybe I'll at least be better at this than I am at running the shop. Honestly? I've been so frazzled that I'll take whatever small victory I can get."

"You've been here a few days now. I say it's time you made some friends. Other than Sunny Sunshine, of course."

Both women laughed as they headed toward the front of the store. A blur of movement caught Summer's eye, and she was pleasantly surprised to spot her mysterious helper from the day before. *Ben.*

She wanted to call out, but her voice caught her throat, so she settled on a wave instead.

Rather than returning her greeting though, he quickly retreated down the nearest aisle and out of view.

Summer frowned.

Maisie put a hand on her shoulder. "So you've already met Ben, I take it?"

"Yeah, and I thought we had made friends, but…"

"That's Ben for you." Maisie sighed and fixed her eyes on the place where Ben had stood just seconds before. "He has the kindest heart, but life has been unfair to him, and now he's a bit… How do I put it? Gun shy. Oh, that's an awful way to say it, considering… But I really shouldn't be telling you his life story. Poor guy's had a hard enough time as it is. Anyway, I'm sure you did make friends, and, well, this is a small town. Seems I can't say that enough about Sweet Grove…But, really, you're destined to run into each other again. Maybe next time he won't be able to make such a fast getaway. Ben is a sweetheart. He just needs a little extra… *Reassurance*."

Well, that was an earful. Summer found herself torn between wondering what had happened to make Ben so skittish and contemplating whether it would be worth the effort to befriend someone who needed so much extra coaxing.

"One for the road," Maisie shouted as she threw an apple at Summer. By some miracle, Summer actually managed to catch the unexpected projectile before it could bounce off her chest and fall to the ground.

"Did you know that the Sweet Grove our town was named for is actually an *apple* grove? Yeah, Golden Delicious just like that one. You won't find better apples anywhere in the country. I don't care what those orchards in New England try to claim. Nothing quite as sweet as the Texas soil and nothing quite as delicious as that there apple." She nodded toward the fruit in Summer's hand.

"Hey, I was wondering how the town got its name. Thanks for the history lesson," she said and then bit down into the sweet fruit and sighed as its delicious juices flooded her taste buds.

Maisie walked over and handed her a small paper bag filled with Golden Delicious and other varieties of apples. "Now, my dear, you're fully initiated. So come on out and celebrate with us. Thursday is karaoke night at the Rusty Nail. The girls and I never miss it, and now that you're here and have been initiated into the Sweet Grove ways, you're one of us too. Meet us there at eight? I won't take no for an answer, so you might as well agree right now."

Summer bobbed her head and thanked Maisie for the invite. She could think of nothing she'd like more than to make a few new friends, especially friends who wouldn't run away whenever she tried to say hello.

Before heading back to her car, she took one last glance around small grocery store. But Ben was nowhere to be found.

Chapter 5

Ben had spent the rest of that day chastising himself for not returning Summer's friendly greeting. Why couldn't he just smile and say hello? They'd spent a nice couple of hours together the afternoon before. He'd enjoyed his time in her company, and it seemed that she had liked talking with him as well. She was clearly grateful for his help, and the smile that spread across her face when she spotted him across the store made it clear she was happy to run into him again.

So then why had he run away? *Sigh.*

No matter how hard he tried, he just couldn't answer that question for himself.

Later that day, Maisie had asked him if he was all right, and he'd said that everything was fine, that he just had a lot of work to do. She eyed him suspiciously but didn't press him any further. Of course, then he had to spend the rest of his shift keeping himself as busy as possible so as not to invite any more unwanted questions.

All the while, he couldn't shake Summer from his mind – not just how terribly he'd messed up, but also her smile, her touch, her kindness, and especially the way being with her had made him feel. Here was a woman who was completely new to town. She didn't know his history, which meant she didn't act stilted around him the way the others so often did. Despite the general panic as they tried to catch up with all the orders at Morning Glory's, their conversations had been effortless, natural, and honestly, the best Ben had had in years. Sure, they'd focused mainly on the tasks that needed to be done, but she treated him like a hero, like he was the only one who could save her from the unfortunate mess she'd made.

And he loved that.

Back and forth he went between happy thoughts of the girl who'd finally broken through his heart's many barriers, and unhappy thoughts of how he himself had behaved that morning. Not even the library could provide adequate distraction when he went there after work to find a new topic to study. He tried the old-fashioned card catalog and the newer digitized computer system. He browsed at random through the stacks, and even asked Sally for her suggestions. But nothing held his interest.

Well, nothing other than Summer...

What if he were to swing by the flower shop and pretend he had a new order from Maisie? Would she believe him? Would that be enough of an excuse? And what would he say if she asked why he had run away from her that morning?

Even though thinking on his feet was obviously not his strong suit, if he tried to force himself to work out all the details beforehand, he'd probably never find the nerve to speak to her again. So he said good-bye to Sally and left without any books to keep him company as he took the short walk toward Morning Glory's.

You can do this. She already likes you. Just say hello, place your order, and ask if you can offer any further help. Easy. That's all he managed to tell himself before his insecurities took over once more.

Why did the thought of seeing her again make him so excited and so nervous all at the same time? He'd never felt this way before, or at least not in a long time. He thought back to freshman year in high school when he had first developed his crush on Elise Nelson. They'd even gone to the homecoming dance together and a couple dates after that. But, as it turned out, a couple of fourteen-year-olds didn't know the first thing about love, and while he liked Elise just fine, they weren't necessarily good together. Not in *that* way at least.

Is that how it would be with Summer too, once the initial excitement of this new attraction wore off? Or would it be different now that he was an adult, now that he knew himself better—now that he had so little else that made him happy in life?

Would it be better to know now whether things could or couldn't work, or should he do whatever it took to cling to the glorious fantasy of *what if?* This particular question terrified him—so much that he hung his head and turned away just before reaching the block where the flower shop sat.

He wasn't ready for this. He hadn't asked for it…

Or had he?

Ben thought back to the desperate prayer he had made and briefly wondered whether it had been heard. Too many questions, not enough answers. It all made Ben's head spin.

Sometimes he just wished he could turn his brain off for the day and be happy like everyone else, but then he realized that this is exactly what his mother had done with the help of liquor. And that it was actually the very *last* thing he wanted for himself.

No, he needed to stay sharp in order to protect them both, even though sometimes it felt that his own mind was conspiring against him.

By the time he turned into his driveway, he had decided that he would lose himself in a Netflix binge that night. Maybe a lighthearted romantic comedy. Perhaps an Adam Sandler movie. He was going to keep daydreaming about Summer no matter what he put on, so he might as well give himself some good material to work with. Actually, he was kind of excited to kick back and browse through all the choices.

"Mom! I'm home!" he called as he walked through the kitchen and thrust open the pantry.

"Mom?" He shouted again as he popped a bag of popcorn into the microwave and watched the turntable spin. When she didn't answer, he tromped over to her room and knocked on the closed door.

Still no answer.

Okay, now he was worried.

That night, Summer slipped into the flirty party dress that she had packed on the off chance she'd find a reason to wear it during her stay in the small, sleepy town. She teased her dark curls and stacked her arms with bangles a friend had brought her from India. A quick coat of dark red lipstick and she was ready for whatever the night brought her way.

Maisie found her the moment she walked through the doors of the Rusty Nail. "My, don't you look like a million bucks? Turn, turn! Let's see the whole thing."

Summer's metallic toned skirt floated around her, making beautiful waves through the air as she spun.

A woman she hadn't yet met reached over and caressed one of Summer's curls. "I am so jealous of that gorgeous hair of yours. My hair won't even hold a ponytail—let alone a perm— and you have all this beautiful natural bounce."

Maisie laughed and pulled her friend away from Summer. "Settle down, she just got here. You're going to scare the poor thing off! Summer, this is Jennifer."

Summer smiled and nodded, noting how uncomfortable Jennifer looked in her heeled shoes. "Nice to meet you. Thanks for having me out tonight."

"Don't mind me. I spend my whole day in the company of kids, and sometimes I forget that it's okay to act like a grown-up." She tittered and saddled Summer with an unexpected, but affectionate, hug.

Maisie rolled her eyes and shook her head. "She's like the kid sister I never had."

"But, boy, would I have liked to grow up with all those handsome brothers of yours!" Jennifer added.

"Don't get me started on my brothers," Maisie said with another eye roll. "Anyway, Summer here is running Morning Glory's while Iris is on her cruise. Jennifer owns the daycare center over on Cypress, and she also serves as the Sunday school teacher at the church. So like she said, sometimes she forgets how to be an adult. But we love her for it! Karaoke nights wouldn't be the same without her. Heck, *life* wouldn't be the same without her."

Jennifer blushed and reached in for another hug, this time from Maisie. "Aww, thank you, Maze."

A fourth woman joined them. "Okay, what did I miss? Who's the new girl? Hey, wait. I know you! We met the other day at Morning Glory's. You're Iris's niece! Summer, right?"

Summer recognized the tall, lively blonde at once. "Hi, Elise. Yeah, that's me. Did your friend like the flowers?"

"Oh, Kristina? She's actually just parking the car now. So you can ask her yourself. I just know you two are going to get along great." Elise leaned into the group and lowered her voice several notches. "Before I forget, Kristina got some less-than-great news from the doctor. I know she'll explain everything herself, but before she gets here, I just wanted to ask if we could all pass on the drinks and the greasy food tonight. She can't have any of that anymore, and I want to make sure we show our support, so she doesn't... Hey! Over here, Kristina!"

A beautiful, plus-sized woman wearing a sequined top and black slacks came over to the group. Unlike the other women of Sweet Grove, her skin was the color of dark honey and her features were full and sensual. She smiled, but Summer could tell she had just recently been crying. "Hello, everyone," she said with a small wave. "Oh, someone new! Hi, I'm Kristina Rose, Kristina Rose Maher. How do you do?"

They all went through a quick round of introductions again and then snagged a table near the stage.

"So you girls do this every week?" Summer asked as the bartender delivered a tray of lemon waters to the women.

"Every single week since Jennifer here turned twenty-one. Wouldn't miss it for the world," Elise explained. She then threw a questioning glance Kristina Rose's way.

Kristina sighed and prodded at the lemon in her glass, using her straw. She tried to smile, but instead she let out a choked sob. Everyone, including Summer, rushed to give her hugs—to show their support before they even knew what they were supporting.

"Would you rather *I* told them?" Elise asked as she rubbed her friend's shoulder.

"No," Kristina said. "I need to get used to talking about this. After all, I'll have to tell everyone at work and church and everywhere else. If I can't find a way to tell my closest friends, how will I explain it to strangers down the road? This is something that's going to change my entire life…"

"Krissy, you're kind of starting to worry me here. Do you have… Oh, I can't even say it! Do you have…?" Maisie struggled to ask.

Jennifer dropped her voice to a whisper, but everyone already knew the word before she could voice it aloud. "Kristina, are you trying to tell us that you have *cancer*?"

Kristina shook her head. This time her smile was real as she tried to comfort her worried friends. "Not cancer. Just diabetes. The doctor said that I need to have gastric bypass surgery in order to get better, since I haven't been able to lose the weight on my own and the diabetes is pretty severe already. He's given me a couple months to prepare for the operation and to practice my new diet. But then I'm going to have to have the surgery, and I'm really scared about it. I've never been cut open before, not even for my appendix or tonsils or anything. And they're starting with my stomach? Talk about an organ I don't trust. How do I know I'll make it through and wake up happier and healthier and skinnier when it's all over?"

"Oh, honey," Maisie said. "You don't know. None of us ever know. That's part of life, but we'll all be praying for you. Right, girls?"

They all nodded enthusiastically, even Summer who didn't typically pray but would if it helped her new friend.

"I'll get the youth group into a prayer circle for you," Elise offered. "You know they all love you. We all love you. You're going to be fine. Sometimes you just have to take that leap of faith and count on God to catch you. This could be the start of a whole new, wonderful life. You just have to get through this short scary part first, but we'll all be here to help!"

Everyone nodded again.

"Thanks, guys." Kristina dabbed at her eyes with a cocktail napkin. "And don't think I didn't notice that none of you ordered drinks. That's really sweet, but you don't have to hold back on my account."

"Yes we do," Jennifer said. "We drink too much anyway. Let's hear what we all sound like singing sober for a change."

"Uh-oh," Maisie wailed. "Maybe count me out then. I don't think anyone wants to hear that. What about you, Summer? Have you done karaoke before?"

She thought back to the party she and her friends had thrown to celebrate their high school graduation, and she couldn't help but smile as she remembered performing a spirited rendition of *It's Raining Men* with a group of her closest girlfriends. Had she grown up in Sweet Grove, she could easily imagine having these same women at her side for that performance and forming just as tight-knit a circle of friends.

But not too many people stayed put after graduation where Summer came from. No, it wasn't like here. Her former classmates were scattered all across the country, which at least meant she would likely have a friend no matter where she chose to take a job and build her life. Then again, Summer never seemed to have any trouble making friends.

"I've been known to grace a stage once or twice in my life," Summer answered. "In fact, I think I'll kick things off for us tonight. Just promise you won't abandon me when you hear how terrible my singing voice is." She laughed at herself and used her palms to push herself up from the table, then strode confidently toward the stage.

"Looks like we have our opening act," the emcee crowed. "And ladies and gentlemen of the Rusty Nail, we're in for a real treat. Because it's none other than Sweet Grove's newest out-of-towner. Let's make her feel welcome, shall we? Give it up for..." He leaned toward Summer with an embarrassed smile and capped his hand over the mic as he spoke. "Uh, what's your name, sweetheart?"

Summer grabbed a hold of the mic and brought it close to her lips. "Hi, everyone. I'm Summer Smith. Yes, Iris Smith's niece. And as you already know, I'm new here. But that's not going to stop me from giving you all one heck of a show. DJ, put on *Jesus Take the Wheel.*"

As the opening notes began to play over the loudspeaker, Summer took a deep breath and held it in her stomach. Sure, it wasn't the most upbeat number, but this song meant something special to her. Though she hadn't been raised to believe in God, Jesus, or whomever, she rather liked the idea of someone bigger and stronger—and, okay, invisible—taking over and steering her life in the direction it needed to go. Lord knew she had enough trouble doing it herself. So as she sang the words she knew so well, she infused them with every bit of emotion and hope and meaning she could muster.

When the song ended, her new friends shot to their feet in around of raucous applause. "Bravo! Bravo!" sang Maisie.

"You were wonderful," said Jennifer, patting Summer on the back as she returned to her seat.

"That's one of my favorite songs too," Kristina Rose added.

"Well, I wouldn't want to be the one to follow that," Elise said with a goofy grin. "But you know what? I will anyway."

Everyone laughed and cheered as Elise rose to take the stage, and Summer found herself feeling more and more at home with these new friends, in this new place, and right here at the Rusty Nail.

Unfortunately, not everyone had enjoyed Summer's performance of the famous Carrie Underwood song. A middle-aged woman with shabby blond hair and deep bags under her eyes flew toward their table in a rage. "You were off key! You are off key the whole time!" she cried.

Maisie was quick to come to her rescue. "Susan, calm down. It's fine. We all loved Summer's performance. Give it a rest."

But the woman, who apparently was named Susan, was not easily deterred. "No! I refuse to let such a beautiful song be butchered by such a terrible voice. You have no right—"

This time it was Elise who spoke up, shouting from her place on the small makeshift stage where she stood waiting for her song to start. "No, *you* have no right. You really shouldn't be here, anyway. Do you need me to take you home?"

Jennifer ran up to the stage and whispered something in Elise's ear.

"I don't care," Elise argued loud enough for the entire bar to hear. "I know all her excuses, but if we let every little thing slip, she's never going to get any better."

Jennifer grabbed Elise's wrist and tried to usher her out of the spotlight, her friend shook her off.

"You may be used to outbursts like this, but I expect more. Did you even know I wanted to be a teacher because of you? You could be great like that again, healthy, sober," Elise implored, tears brimming behind her large eyes. "Here, let me take you home."

"I don't need anything from you or anyone else," the drunken woman said. This time Summer realized how slurred the words came out. "Except you." She pointed one shaky finger toward Summer rather dramatically. "You need to apologize for what you did to that song."

Maisie shot her feet, and Summer hoped she wasn't getting ready for a fight. That was the last thing she wanted on her first night out in town. If drama were to ensue, she would be so embarrassed she would hardly be able to handle herself for her remaining weeks. Things were already hard enough at the flower shop. She didn't want her social life to be spoiled as well.

She raised a hand to cut off Maisie before she could take the confrontation any further. "It's okay, really. I know I'm not a great singer, and I love that song too. That's why I picked it. Tell you what, let me take you home and I'll apologize on the way. Deal?"

Susan blew a raspberry, upsetting the loose bangs on her forehead, then walked toward the exit, perhaps agreeing with the plan or perhaps already bored with them.

"Are you sure about this, Summer? I'm happy to take her. You stay and have fun. The night's only just getting started," Maisie insisted.

"It's okay. I want to help. Her name is Susan, right? Do you know where she lives? Can you tell me how to get there?"

"Yes, her name is Susan Davis, and she lives at Seventeen-oh-one May Lane. To get there, you just turn right out of—"

"Actually," Summer said, "I know exactly how to get there." She grabbed up her keys and her purse and followed Ben's mother outside. Well, like it or not, this time he would have to say hello.

Chapter 6

Ben leaped the moment he heard a knock on the hollow front door. Relief flooded him when he saw his mother standing there, thankfully in one piece. But when he saw who was standing next to her, his heart thrummed wildly once again. *Summer.*

"We ran into each other at the Rusty Nail, and I figured she could use a ride home." Summer shook her head. "Hello, Ben. It's nice to see you again." She twisted her hands at her side suggesting maybe she too felt nervous in his company.

"Come on in," Susan said as she shuffled past Ben and made her way to the kitchen.

"Mom…?" Ben began, not knowing exactly what he wanted to ask.

Susan reappeared at his side and nudged him out of the way to allow Summer to enter their home. "It's okay. She already apologized, so I invited her in for a nightcap."

Summer shot him an awkward smile and shrugged, then followed his mother into the house. "Just water, thanks."

Ben couldn't very well retreat in this situation, though this definitely wasn't how he'd imagined the next meeting might start with his dream girl. In fact, seeing her standing there so pure and beautiful next to the harsh nightmare of his everyday reality made him want to scream. He frowned as he glanced around the house and noted the clutter and the mess and the general disorder around them. Then there was his mother, who'd obviously been drinking—and out in public. And he didn't even want to know what she meant when she said Summer had apologized.

"Mind if I join you?" He leaned against the kitchen doorframe, feeling like the worst pickup artist ever.

His mother busily worked on finding a pair of clean glasses while Summer sat tapping her fingers on the old wooden table that had been a staple in their home decor since before Ben had even been born. When neither woman answered, he decided to take a seat himself. *Fake it until you make it, right?*

His feelings for Summer were anything but fake, but his confidence…? Well, he couldn't just sit there ogling her, just as he couldn't leave her captive to the whims of his erratic mother.

"How have you been? I mean, are things at the shop going better?" he asked.

Summer nodded subtly as she watched Susan continue to search the kitchen cabinets. "Oh, as good as they could be, considering. I'll manage to survive one way or another." Her words seemed dismissive, yet she punctuated them with a kind, reassuring smile.

After a few more moments, she raised her voice and craned her neck to look past Ben. "Susan, how is that glass of water coming? Do you need any help?"

His mother sighed. "No clean glasses," she explained. "But I should have a few cold cans of beer in the garage fridge. I'll be right back."

Now Summer was the one to sigh as Ben's mother walked swiftly yet unsteadily toward the garage. Turning to Ben, she whispered, "I get the feeling this isn't a 'sometimes thing' with her."

"Well, she doesn't usually leave the house, but yeah. I'm sorry you got mixed up in this mess."

"Is this why…?" She bit her lip as if that would keep the unspoken words from escaping. "Never mind. Just tell me how I can help."

"It's beyond help. Believe me, I've tried."

"No, I refuse to believe that anyone is a lost cause. Speaking of, umm…where is she?" Susan still hadn't returned from her quick trip to the garage. That was when the TV in her bedroom flared up, bringing with it the sound of an old sitcom rerun. The laugh track jarred Ben's nerves, but he tried not to show his irritation.

"Well, that answers that question," Summer said with a frown. "C'mon." She stood up and pulled Ben to his feet as well, then immediately started rustling through the cabinets as his mother had done just moments before.

"What are you doing?" he asked.

"Looking for any hidden bottles of liquor or wine or whatever. She can't get better if we don't help her. We need to find them and throw them out."

Ben decided not to mention the fact that none of the booze was actually hidden, that in fact he regularly purchased fresh supplies for Susan and that they kept it in plain sight."Let me get you a trash bag," he said, reaching under the sink and pulling out a black, shiny bag.

She didn't hesitate to grab it from him and throw in a mostly empty bottle of Jack. "Thanks."

Ben went to get the bottles his mother kept tucked into the back of the couch cushions and brought them back to Summer, who dunked them in the bag with a triumphant expression.

"I understand the urge to lose yourself in a bottle. Really, I do, but when it gets to this point of not even being able to help yourself, well... You need others to intervene on your behalf." She sighed heavily. "Does she...?" Summer chewed on her lower lip for a moment before rephrasing her question. "Is she ever violent at all?"

Ben shook his head vigorously. "No, no, nothing like that. She just likes to... to forget is all."

"Forget what?" The trash bag drooped toward the floor as Summer silently studied Ben. "Maybe I shouldn't pry. I just want to help."

"It's okay. If you haven't heard about what happened with my brother already, it's only a matter of time. Someone is bound to tell you eventually. Might as well be me."

Summer set the bag down on the floor and seated herself at the table once again. "What is it?"

Ben sat down with her and stared at the floor as he spoke. He'd hate to see that light leave Summer's eyes once she learned the awful truth about him and his family, but it was only a matter of time. "About five years ago," he started, risking a quick glance up at her.

She smiled reassuringly, so he continued. "My brother Stephen shot himself over on Main Street. In broad daylight, no less. He died instantly. Didn't even feel much, if any, pain, the doctor said. But ever since then, my mom has felt nothing but pain. So she started drinking, lost her job. My dad left, and that left only me to take care of us both."

"Oh, Ben. I'm so sorry! I had no idea!" Her voice was kind, but Ben didn't dare look up at her face yet. If he could just hang on to the easiness between them for a little longer, perhaps everything would be all right. She reached over and patted his back as if to comfort him for having such a sucky life.

"How could you have?" he continued. "Anyway, I know I shouldn't, but it's easier just to buy her the booze than to have the same fight every single day, you know?"

"That's what my mom thought too," Summer whispered. "But he hit her anyway. Hit her if she didn't bring him something to drink. Hit her if she did. I couldn't get out of there fast enough once I graduated. My Aunt Iris even offered to let me move in with her here, but I wanted to make my own way. That way, I could never get stuck the way my mom had with my stepdad."

Ben was quiet as Summer continued to speak, but he did at last raise his eyes to meet hers. She stared straight ahead, her gaze unfocused as she recounted the story from her past.

"But funnily enough," she continued with a small sarcastic laugh. "I'm stuck anyway. I'm not trapped by any one person. Just me, myself, and my inability to decide. That's why I came to Sweet Grove this summer. To help my aunt, yes, but also to force myself to finally decide what I want to do with my life. I've been here three days, and the only thing I know for sure is that I *don't* want to be a florist." She laughed again, then let out a long sigh.

"I shouldn't get so down on myself. I don't want to make you feel bad. I just want you to know that I understand in a way. And I'm here if you ever want to talk or to just get away for an hour or two. Okay?"

Ben nodded. "Okay."

So their lives weren't so very different after all. Only Summer had found a way to get out of a bad situation, and Ben had just made his own worse. She still wore a smile on her face, while Ben silently contemplated wrapping a rope around his neck and taking that one last, little step toward death.

But now he was here with this girl, who was both beautiful and kind, damaged yet hopeful. If she could find a way to survive, then maybe he could too.

Summer shot a glowing smile his way and reached out to squeeze his hand before leaping up from her seat and grabbing up the trash bag. "Good, now let's finish cleaning out this stuff."

By some miracle, things were quiet at Morning Glory's that Friday afternoon. The rush from the out-of-town funeral had reached its natural end, and so far not a single customer had come to make any requests of Sweet Grove's new florist.

Sunny Sunshine was a different story altogether. Despite being her Aunt Iris's best friend, her so-called feather baby, the brightly colored little bird didn't seem to care much for Iris's replacement. He screamed and shrieked and even made a noise that sounded a bit like a car alarm. It all gave Summer a wicked headache until she reluctantly draped her jacket over Sunny's travel cage. Hopefully the bird would stay quiet for a few minutes—or at least long enough for the pain killers to do away with Summer's aching head.

Elise swept into the store, her commanding presence immediately filling the place. "So how's business?"

"Slow," Summer said with a shrug. "Sorry I missed your performance last night. How was it?"

"You were a tough act to follow, but at least I didn't get booed off the stage. We missed you after you left. You didn't have to leave so soon, but it was a really nice thing you did for Susan."

"It was the least I could do, seeing as I'm the one who got her all riled up to begin with. Besides, I was happy to be able to help."

"Oh, speaking of music and performances and *happy...*" Elise gave an over-the-top smile as if exulting in her own ostentatiousness. "The concert's tomorrow. Are you going to be able to make it? Pretty much the whole town is going to be there, and I'd love to introduce you around. And, not to brag or anything, but the youth group events are always the most fun. We have a few bands coming from out of town to perform, plus some of our local kids will be taking the stage as well. In a word, *awesome*. It's going to be *awesome*, and I want to spend more time with you too. So go ahead, tell me you'll come."

"Okay, okay." Summer couldn't help but laugh—something she did often around Elise. "Can I bring a friend with me? I happen to have a new friend who is incredibly passionate about music."

Elise scrunched up her nose. "Do you mean Susan?"

Summer nodded. "Well, yeah, and her son, Ben. If everyone's going to be there, then they shouldn't miss it either, right?"

"If you can get them to come, then you'll have accomplished something I've never been able to. I like Ben. In fact, he was my first boyfriend back in high school, and I was in Mrs. Davis's fourth grade class a million years ago. But they've both changed so much, since... I mean—"

"It's okay," Summer broke in. "He told me what happened with Stephen."

"Oh, good. I didn't want to be the one to say it. I'm not a huge fan of gossip. No offense to your Aunt Iris! It's just that when gossip works its way through my youth group, drama always inevitably follows. Teenagers, right?"

They both laughed, but the previous lightness had drained from the room.

"So you and Ben were an item, huh?" Summer asked at last. If the situation was awkward already, she may as well learn a thing or two.

Elise nodded and winked in a gesture that wasn't unlike a rap star. "Jealous?"

"What? No, just curious." Summer walked over to the card carousel in an effort to look nonchalant.

Elise joined her and began thumbing through the section with all the funny kitten photos.

"So…you and Ben?"

"Ancient history." Elise plucked a card from the stand, opened it, then laughed when the noisemaker inside let out a caterwauling meow. She closed the card again and fixed her gaze firmly on Summer. "*You* and Ben?"

Summer turned as red as whichever flowers were red. Other than roses, she honestly didn't know. All she knew was that waves of heat crashed into her cheeks, and her heart fluttered in her chest. "I don't actually know," she admitted. *Change of topic, change of topic!* She desperately searched her mind until she came up with the perfect redirect.

"Hey," she said, traipsing back over to the main counter and placing a hand on the cooler door. "How are you with flowers? Come help me make an arrangement for Susan. She deserves to have something pretty in her life. Wouldn't you say?"

"Oh, man," Elise teased. "You've got it bad. So, so bad."

Summer opened her mouth to argue, but what was the point in denying it? She *did* like Ben, perhaps too much for just a summer crush. Her feelings were bound to fade eventually, weren't they? She didn't know if they would, and she also didn't know if she wanted them to.

For now at least she could focus on making a beautiful—or at least as close to beautiful as she was capable of—bouquet. And then what?

Chapter 7

On Friday afternoon, Ben went straight to the library after finishing his shift at the Sweet Grove market. He'd finished all his work quickly that day, so Maisie had offered to let him to leave an hour early without forfeiting any pay. Normally, he'd refuse and find some other task to keep himself busy, but on this day he decided to say yes. Even Maisie seemed surprised when he hung up his product scanner and clocked out for the day.

And now that he found himself in the familiar company of Sally and all her many books, he decided to study up on the history of psychology rather than continuing Russian Tsarist history. Naturally, he avoided Freud, having no desire to blame all his shortcomings on his mother any more than he already did.

Instead, he began reading about Maslow and the hierarchy of needs. He liked that the hierarchy was represented by a pyramid. He did not like that he had only two-ish blocks accounted for, which wasn't very good, considering most people had at least three. He got hung up on the whole "love and belonging" level of Maslow's motivational model. Did that mean he'd be happier if he put his discomfort aside and tried harder to form actual friendships? The book cited friends, sports, clubs, church, even gangs as good ways of getting his needs met in this level—all pretty obvious, really. It also referenced, umm, romantic relationships. Well, if that's what the book wanted, who was he to disagree?

Besides, once he mastered that block, he could move on to esteem and finally self-actualization. If he did *that*, he would be at the top of the pyramid; he'd become the highest, best version of himself—the version Summer deserved.

Then again, Maslow's theories dated back to World War II and had since been called into question. Still, Ben liked the idea of being able to take measured steps toward self-improvement. What if it really were that easy? What if he could take a good, long look at each area of his life, intentionally add things back in—things he'd once had before Stephen ripped his family apart? What if doing this would mean he could finally make something of himself, pursue his dreams, become a man worthy of a woman like Summer?

She'd had her own fair share of troubles. Sure, she hadn't divulged much, but he knew enough to see that Summer had triumphed over her hardships—whether or not she believed she had. If Summer could do it, then couldn't he with a little extra knowledge and encouragement?

According to Maslow, he could start his road to recovery by simply making a friend or two. That worked, seeing as he definitely didn't have the time or the money to seek out a therapist. Even if he did have that kind of spare cash just lying around, he's see to it that his mother got help first.

Ahh, money. It always came back to money. Not having enough of it, wanting more of it, that kind of thing.

"How's it going today, Ben?" Sally strode through the stacks then took a seat across from him at the small table.

"Good, good. I'm just reading up on Abraham Maslow. Are you familiar with him?"

"I remember him from my Intro to Psychology course. The Humanist school of thought, am I right?"

"Exactly. Man, you are like a sponge, Sally. How is it that you know everything about everything?"

A self-satisfied grin spread across her face. "I read a lot. Just like you," she pointed out.

He put a piece of notebook paper in the old psychology textbook to hold his spot, and shut it. "How has your day been so far?"

"My day?" she gasped. "You never ask me about *my day*. What's gotten into you, Ben?"

"I don't know," he lied, not yet ready to divulge the seriousness of his crush on Summer. "But I like it."

"If it's that book, then I think I'll borrow it when you're done."

"Here, take it now." He nudged it across the table, and Sally caught it before it could slide off. "I'm going to go grab a book on Jung to see what he has to say about the human brain."

Sally stood, hugging the book to her chest as if it were a precious child and not a bunch of outdated words and theories. "Well, thanks. Hey, do you maybe want to talk about it when I'm done? Kind of like an impromptu book club?"

"Sounds good. Thanks, Sally." Ben stood too and started back toward the small-town library's tiny psychology section. He'd have all these books read in no time, especially if he checked some out and took them home with him.

"Wait. Ben?"Sally called after him.

"Yeah?" He turned to study her. She was really quite pretty with her dark hair and fair skin, and she'd always been so nice to him. If he weren't completely enamored of Summer, then maybe one day he could have found love with Sally. It would have been easy to make a life with her, to learn new things side by side, to have somebody to kiss and hold. A relationship with Sally would be built on pragmatism, shared interests, but not passion.

And Ben didn't want a slow burn kind of romance. He loved the fireworks he saw whenever he so much as thought of breezy, beautiful Summer.

"Whatever has you feeling like this," Sally continued. "Make sure you don't let it go. I don't know if I've ever seen you this upbeat. And, well, I really like it. You have such a nice smile. Try to show it more often."

Ben blushed. "I will, thank you."

Sally hoisted the book in the air. "Off to go *wo*man the front desk. Have a good night, Ben."

"Good night, Sally." Ben smiled to himself as he turned back toward the shelves and ran his thumb over a line of books that were crammed tightly together on the lowest shelf.

"Hi, Ben." A voice came from above him. Not Sally's, but…

"Summer! Hi!" He shot to his feet, his search for the new book quickly forgotten.

She gave him a hug then quickly pulled away. "Maisie told me I might find you here, and look. She was right. Thanks for everything last night. It helped to talk things out."

"Thank you for taking care of my mom. You don't even know her, but you still wanted to help. I love that about you."

She blushed at the word *love*, and Ben realized too late what he'd said. Love already? Infatuation maybe, but surely not love. But he'd already said it. If he took it back now, then that would just call more attention to his little Freudian slip. Darn, he hadn't managed to escape the old mother-lover, after all.

"Um, thank you." Summer tucked a stray tendril of hair behind her ear. "I actually have a request for you, if you don't mind."

"No, go ahead."

"Would you please, umm… Well, would you mind inviting me over to your place for dinner?"

"I would… what?"

"I want to make dinner for you and your mom and get to know you both better. Would that be okay?"

"Yes, of course. That would be awesome."

"So you'll invite me?"

"Yes, of course," he said.

Summer tapped her foot as she waited for him to catch up.

"Oh, would you like to come over to my house for dinner tonight?"

She blushed again. "Yes, please! I have everything just about ready, I just needed the invite first. Would it be okay if I came by at six?"

"Yeah, that would be awesome," he said again. Man, he really needed to learn some new words. Maybe when he was done with psychology he could read the dictionary.

"Well, great. Thank you. I'll see you then." Summer tucked her hair behind her ears again, then bobbed off toward the exit, leaving Ben to contemplate whether this was a date—and whether he'd asked her on it, or she'd asked him.

He'd said yes. Of course he'd said yes. Summer hadn't expected to be turned down, but she also hadn't expected to feel butterfly wings beat in her chest the moment Ben smiled and asked her to dinner as she'd requested.

Okay, so maybe she had *a bit* of a crush. That much had been obvious the second she'd received the news of his former relationship with Elise. Oh, was she jealous! But that had been years ago, and besides, Summer was in no place to start something new. As the saying went, she was just passing through, just in Sweet Grove for a season. Before anyone knew it, the leaves would be turning orange and she would be driving off into the sunset.

At least she hoped it would go that way. More and more it looked as though she'd end up working at a temp agency until she could finally, actually, make up her mind about what she wanted to do with her life. But the more she dilly-dallied about making the momentous decision, the more immobilized with fear she became. What if she chose wrong?

If she refused to choose then at least some hope would remain, right?

No.

That was ridiculous. Utter nonsense.

Tonight she could enjoy her time with Ben and Susan, and tomorrow she could resume her soul searching—or rather job searching. Well, she would do something productive. She didn't have much choice.

But that would come tomorrow. Tonight she had to prepare dinner, and if she didn't pay attention to her cooking, she would likely burn the bisque or over-toss the salad, provided such a thing were actually possible.

Good food could do wonders for the mind and body. Some people swore a nice slice of chocolate cake or a homemade batch of mac and cheese could brighten even the gloomiest of days, but Summer believed that healthier was always better when it came to food. Eating green, leafy things made her feel good on the inside and glow on the outside, and she wanted to share that with Susan. And, okay, Ben too.

Getting sober was no easy task, and she wanted to do her part to help Susan be successful. Partially because she needed to do something useful to feel halfway good about herself, and partly for Ben. She had a crush, after all, and if she helped him save his mother, then maybe she'd always have a bit of his heart—even after she had long since left Sweet Grove.

She missed the healthy, yummy, crunchy foods of SoCal. Food was so different here in Texas, and her stomach hadn't quite made peace with that yet. She'd never been much of a cook, but she wanted to try to make something nice to bring over to the Davises' that night.

After all, she was the one who had invited herself. Now it was time to make the best possible impression with her cooking, her conversation, her looks—all of it.

As she slipped into her favorite summer dress and a pair of strappy sandals, she reminded herself over and over again that she was there to help, not to flirt. But still… she wasn't sure she actually believed it.

Chapter 8

This time, when a soft knock sounded on Ben's front door, he was prepared. Still, as soon as he opened the door, the sight of Summer waiting there in a soft spring dress sent shivers straight through him. He noted a delicate chain around her neck with a heart-shaped locket that fell just beneath her collarbone and briefly wondered whose pictures might be inside.

"Hi," she said with a sweet smile and a quick bashful duck of her head.

"Hi."

Had she gotten dressed up for this evening, or did she always put such pride into her appearance? Ben ran his palms through his hair, then motioned for their guest to come inside. As soon as he and Summer had made their plans that afternoon, he'd rushed home to clean the house up as much as possible, but he'd failed to take such efforts on his own appearance. A mistake, he now realized.

"I hope you like what I made for dinner. It's a little different, but I figured not much could surprise you, seeing that you work in the grocery store where I bought all the ingredients." She shifted her weight from one foot to the other as she talked. "Besides I think it will be good for Susan to have a fresh, organic meal. Good for you, too."

"I'm sure it's awesome." Darn, there was that word again. Yup, he'd definitely be hitting the dictionary section the next time he went to the library. "Here, let me take that from you," he said. "Mom is just finishing setting the table. C'mon, I'll show you in."

"Well, aren't you a vision!" Susan set down the last of the silverware and came to give Summer a hug. "Thank you for the flowers."

"Flowers?" Ben couldn't stop himself from asking. He also did his best to avoid calculating the last time his mother had hugged him so warmly. He'd be jealous if he didn't like Summer so much himself. Hey, whatever got her here worked just fine for him.

Finally, Mom has found a way to be of use. Wait, how can I even think such a thing? I'm a bad, bad son.

The women continued their banter, unaware of the dark thoughts running through Ben's brain. "Oh, good, you got them!" Summer squealed.

Everyone glanced over to the table where, in the center, a fat floral arrangement sat.

"I remember you said you liked gardening and I figured they could be the final piece of my apology for the song."

Both women laughed, and Ben remained confused.

Susan placed a hand on Summer's shoulder, as if she needed the other woman to help her keep standing. "Oh, c'mon now. I'm sorry I gave you such a hard time about that. I was having a rough day."

"I understand. I'm not the best singer or florist for that matter, but I try my best to do whatever makes me happy."

"That's a lesson we could both learn from you. Right, Ben?" Now she grabbed Ben and pulled him into her side. He hated when she did that.

Ben nodded uncomfortably.

"I hope this isn't rude, but I'm starved. Mind if we plate up while we talk?" Even though the question was addressed to his mother, Summer shot a shy glance Ben's way.

He nodded again.

"Ben, c'mon, help her out, would you?" Susan said, embarrassing Ben once again.

Summer also turned red. "It's okay, I've got it. It's better I do it, so I can explain what everything is. You both take a seat." Another shy glance toward Ben, a smile.

He knew he should pay better attention to her explanations of what each dish entailed, but he quickly found himself lost in her smile, the soft cadence of her words, the gentle movements of her hands as she served up each dish. Soon his plate was full, and Summer took a seat across from him.

"Now it's time to dig in. As I said, the roasted fennel is my favorite." She speared the vegetables with her fork and popped a big bite into her mouth.

Hungry as he was that evening, Ben had to force himself to look away from Summer and onto his plate of brightly colored foods. He followed Summer's example and started with the fennel. Was it bad that he'd spent years stocking such vegetables but had never actually tried them? Sure, they were only in season for a short while and the supply was always meager so as to make space for the other, more popular foods, but *wow*.

As he gnashed the fleshy vegetable with his teeth, an unexpected symphony of flavors played out on his tongue.

"Do you like it?" Summer asked, looking from him to Susan and back again.

He nodded and smiled at Summer to let her know how much he enjoyed it without being so uncouth as to talk with his mouth open, and immediately took another bite.

His mother, who very rarely found herself in the company of anyone but Ben, didn't take such precautions. "Yummo!" she said enthusiastically. "Where'd you learn to cook like this?"

"Well, I have an app that walked me through everything. Looks like it deserves a five-star rating. I'll shoot you the link later, so you can try it out too."

Ben and his mother couldn't afford smart phones; he silently prayed Susan wouldn't mention that. He also knew what the organic vegetables cost and wasn't sure they could fit them into their budget. Luckily, Susan said none of this and returned to focusing on the food in front of her.

They ate in silence for a while as Ben wondered how he could better break the ice with Summer— beyond the constant nodding and declaring everything she did "awesome." He also wondered what she would surprise him with next and what other wonderful things were just outside his front door simply waiting to be discovered.

Okay, *yes*, Summer wanted to talk with Ben, but somehow it was easier to focus on Susan, the food—

anything but her undeniable attraction to the quiet loner of Sweet Grove. Besides, she didn't want to mess up and accidentally flirt with him right there in front of his mom. Man, it was like they were in high school again—the butterflies, the stolen glances, *the chaperone.*

But as much as Summer wanted to get to know Ben better, she also liked Susan and wanted to help. There was no way she would mess up and accidentally fall in love with *Susan,* after all.

The three of them chewed in silence for a while and Summer searched her brain for an appropriate topic of conversation. Somehow their bites had become synchronized like some sort of strange kitchen dance. *Ah-ha, music!*

"So I already know you love Carrie Underwood," she said to Susan, laying her fork down. "What other types of music do you enjoy?"

"Sorry again for that outburst. I honestly can't even remember much of that night." Susan laughed at herself, but the glint in her eye betrayed a deeper, hidden pain.

"It's okay. It brought us all together, right?" She caught Ben staring at her and heat rose to her cheeks. Was he staring at her because of the awkwardness or because he liked looking at her? Did that mean he had a bit of a crush on her too? *Gaah,* they really were in high school again.

Susan smiled and took another bite of couscous, leaving Summer's question unanswered.

Ben jumped in to keep the conversation from getting off track. "Mom used to sing in the church choir. She was the lead soprano actually, before…" He grimaced and quickly changed the topic. "I mean, she likes all kinds of music. Country, oldies, pop, everything except maybe rap."

"Why do you say I don't like rap?" Susan asked between bites.

"Okay, so all kinds of music then." Ben laughed. "No exceptions."

Summer waited for him to ask about her interests, but he didn't. So she tried a new line of conversation.

"I already know Ben works at Maisie's market. What do you do for work, Susan?"

"Nothing. I got fired."

"Oh, I'm so sorry. Was this recent?"

"About three years ago. Said I drink too much."

Oh, no. She was asking all the wrong questions. Her attempts at being nice were actually making the whole evening even more uncomfortable for everyone, especially poor Susan who now kept her eyes glued firmly on her nearly empty plate.

Ben wiped his lips with a paper napkin, then again answered in Susan's place. "She, um, used to be a fourth grade teacher. The kids really loved her too."

Susan sighed. "*Ahh, memories.* The whole reason I drink to begin with. If you two don't mind, I think I'll just head to bed now."

"I'm sorry, I didn't mean to…"

"It's not your fault, Summer. Thank you for bringing dinner. It was great. Right, Mom?"

"Yes, thank you and goodnight."

They both watched Susan pad out of the kitchen. Neither spoke until the bedroom door clicked shut behind her.

"I'm willing to bet she has a stash in there that we didn't find the other night," Ben said at last.

"Oh, I hope I didn't…"

"You were *awesome*, Summer. I can't remember the last time we sat down for a meal together or had company for that matter. I know you want to help and you are helping. It's just that… Well, her problems require more than one nice evening if they're ever going to get solved. Know what I mean?"

"I do, but thanks for saying that." She nodded and gave him a playful jab on the arm. Okay, he'd told her she was awesome at least a dozen times that day, did that mean he liked her every bit as much as she liked him? Or did that just mean he didn't have many other words to express himself? No, Ben seemed like a smart guy, which meant...

"Again, really awesome of you. Thank you," Ben said and then shook his head. "I mean, it was nice, good, any other word. Though it *was* pretty awesome too."

"I know what you mean," she said, and she did. Their attraction was definitely mutual. She wrapped her arms around her torso in a self-hug and bit back a yawn. "Man, it's getting late. Would you mind walking me home?"

He quirked an eyebrow at her, drawing attention to his gorgeous emerald gaze. "Didn't you drive?"

"Yeah, but it's not far, and I could really use a bit of fresh air to clear my head. Is it okay if I come back for the car later?"

That way I'll be sure to see you again, she added in her head.

"Let's do it," he answered. "But first..." He went to the coat closet and grabbed a worn zip-up hoodie. "It gets kind of cold out there after the sun sets for the night, so you'd better put this on."

Summer looped an arm through each sleeve, enveloping herself in the piney, clean scent of the boy she now totally admitted she was crazy about. "Thanks. This is *awesome.*"

Chapter 9

Of course, more time with Summer away from his mother's watchful eye suited Ben just fine. He still wasn't entirely sure why she even wanted to give his drunk, ill-mannered mom any of her precious time, but he was certainly glad she continued to come around. As much as Ben liked all the time he was now getting with the girl of his dreams, he also felt guilty that it took an outsider to finally help Susan out of her alcoholic stupor.

The changes were slight, but still progress had been made. Now as he walked with Summer beneath a sky full of shining stars, he wanted to make sure she knew this. "You're really amazing, you know."

"What? Not awesome?" She scrunched her nose up playfully, fixing her gaze on him rather than the sidewalk ahead. Would she stumble and give him the chance to catch her? He kind of hoped so.

"Haha, very funny. But, yes. You're both amazing and awesome, and so many other things in between." If he reached out to grab her hand, would she let him? He decided not to push his luck in that department just yet, given how thick he was already laying on the flattery.

"My mom," he continued. "It's amazing that you are so set on helping her. She's really perked up since meeting you." And so have I, he added internally, but did not say aloud. She already knew he was damaged, but it was probably too soon for her to find out just how broken he was on the inside.

"I hope so. I mean, I really do want to help. I kind of wish I'd majored in psychology or something like that instead of communications. Do you think I would be a good therapist? Maybe I should go back to school."

"You would be great. I mean you already are... awesome."

"Yeah, I think you've mentioned that." She laughed but didn't give him any more of a hard time about it.

"I like psychology too," he said when her laughter abated. "In fact, I was studying up on it when you found me in the library this afternoon."

"Oh? I didn't realize. Is that what you go to school for? Are you only back home for the summer?"

"No, I'm here for the... well, always. No school, even though I'd really liked to have gone. I had to stay here to take care of Mom."

"You're a good son," she said.

"I wish that were true. Most days I find myself resenting her, resenting my brother."

"Were you two close before he...?"

"No," he said through clenched teeth. He needed to get this conversation back on track and fast, but he also owed it to Summer to be honest with her. He couldn't be sure given the dark sky, but Ben thought he saw Summer frown.

"We don't have to talk about it if you don't want to."

"No, you deserve to know. It will help you understand us a bit better." He took a slow, deep breath. "I remember finding out about *the accident*—that's what they called it 'an accident'. Nobody wanted to admit that Stephen had intentionally shot himself in the face. I was in my junior year of high school. They called me to the office midday, and I actually worried that I was in trouble. But then my mom was there to get me and told me everything. That may have been the last time I saw her sober, actually. My dad gave her space for a few months, but after a while he would start to fight whenever she reached for another drink. And awhile after that, he just up and left. I haven't seen the deadbeat since."

Summer drifted closer to him, as if his sorrow had its own gravitational pull. "That's awful. It must have been so hard on her."

He nodded and thought again about reaching for her hand, but, no, he didn't want her to feel obligated to be kind to him. He wanted this to be real, because so little else in his life actually was. "Hard on us all. She lost her job shortly after that, and the drinking got even worse. Luckily, by then I was close to graduation and was able to transition to working full time at the market. It was only ever supposed to be an after-school job. I had a full ride to UT in Austin. It would have covered room and board as well as tuition, but it wouldn't have paid the mortgage on our house. It wouldn't have taken care of my mom. So I turned it down and stayed here. Just until she gets better, I told myself. But she hasn't gotten better yet, and I hate to say it, but I'd kind of given up trying until…"

Oh, to heck with it. Ben reached for Summer's hand and laced his fingers between hers. She gave his hand a soft squeeze, but didn't let go.

"Until *you*," he said bravely at the exact same time Summer said, "This is me."

What timing!

She let go of his hand as they walked up onto the porch of a quirky little ranch house with a whole army of garden gnomes placed around the front lawn.

"Thanks again for everything," he said.

"I had a good time tonight," she said, and then, "Ben?"

"Yes?"

"Would you like to come inside and have some tea with me?"

Why did you invite him in for tea? Summer asked herself. *Is this what you call not getting involved? You are going to hurt him if you're not careful. So be careful already! Behave!*

"So what kind of tea do you have?" Ben asked, taking the bait she'd tossed his way.

"Umm, actually, I don't know. Let me check the cupboards." She strode into the kitchen and hoped she'd find all the fixings she needed to make a nice cup of tea. Aunt Iris was forever drinking herbal this and English breakfast that. Summer herself had always been more of a coffee person, but Ben didn't need to know that. If he found out the tea was just an excuse for continuing their conversation, for getting him to stay a bit longer than he otherwise might have…

"Ah-ha! I knew Aunt Iris wouldn't let me down. Earl Grey okay?"

He shook his head, "Yeah, I mean, I'm not much of a tea drinker, but I'm sure it will be delicious."

She found the kettle and filled it up then put it over the electric cook top. She thought about what she might like to ask Ben and whether maybe—just maybe—it could be okay to flirt a little bit in the process.

Then it hit her. "Oh, shoot!"

"What? What's wrong?" Ben shot to his feet and glanced around the tiny house's open floor plan.

"There's this thing tomorrow, and I wanted to invite your mom, but I forgot."

"What kind of thing?"

"A concert at the church. Do you think she'd want to come? Elise invited me, and it sounds like a lot of fun." She watched for a reaction at the mention of his ex-girlfriend, but there wasn't one.

"She used to love singing at the church. I'm sure she'd come along if you asked her. She doesn't usually leave the house unless someone invites her to go somewhere, and as the years pass, fewer and fewer people do. I think that's why she's enjoyed meeting you so much. You look at her with fresh eyes."

"I'd like you to come too. If that's all right."

"Yeah. I mean, *yeah.*"

Just then the tea kettle whistled. Summer grabbed it off the hot stove and moved it onto a tiny parrot-shaped trivet as she searched around for a pair of mugs.

"Do you mind if I ask you a kind of personal question?" She put a tea bag in each mug and poured hot water in after.

"Shoot."

"How come you ran away from me the other day at the market? I thought we had… I thought we had a good time at the flower shop, but then the very next day you were avoiding me like I was some kind of leper."

Ben sighed and looked away. "That's a good question. Unfortunately, I don't have a very good answer. I was scared, I guess."

"Of me?"

"No, of what I felt when you were around."

She frowned. "I don't get it."

He stood up and walked over to her. Just inches away from her now, he looked down at her from his position about a half foot taller. And like the stars that had just guided her home, they sparkled. The guy's eyes sparkled. Was that the look of love?

"I like you, Summer. A lot," he whispered.

She smiled and handed him a mug of tea. "I like you too, Ben."

"Can I ask you a personal question?"

"Of course." *But not while we're standing this close, it's too risky,* she thought as she bounced back over to the table, doing her best to look happy-go-lucky about it all.

"Why?" Ben cleared his throat, then asked again, "Why do you like me?"

Well, now there's the million-dollar question. She'd been so focused on the fact she liked him, she hadn't even asked herself why. "I don't know. I just do," she said.

He laughed and took a sip of tea. Had she hurt his feelings by not saying more?

"I really do, Ben. I do." She leaned in and gave him a quick peck on the cheek to make sure he understood that.

"Good."

"Good."

And they continued to drink their tea in comfortable silence.

Chapter 10

Ben couldn't stop smiling as he shaved that morning. Last night with Summer had been so freeing. To be able to open up to someone like that and to still feel accepted when the truth had come out—magic. Most of his fears had been laid to rest. Now he just wanted every second of Summer he could soak up while she was in Sweet Grove for the next few months. In fact, he planned to ask her on an official date once the concert was through.

And if the sweet, simple kiss on the cheek she'd given him the night before was any indicator, she would definitely say yes.

Love. Was it too soon to feel his heart fill with tenderness for the woman he'd hardly known a week? If not in love, then at least he was happy—and that was something he'd truly never expected to feel again. Now look at him, going to church—*church!*—of all places.

Although his mother had sung in the choir for years, his father had actively and loudly disapproved. He didn't believe in God, and he didn't approve of his mother trying to force their boys into believing either. That's why he'd always had the choice as to whether or not to attend services. When faced with the option of spending a couple hours sitting quietly or a fun day at the cider mill with his dad and brother, he always chose the latter.

Perhaps if their father had tried a little harder, Stephen could have found comfort in faith, and perhaps that would have saved him in the end. Perhaps, too, Susan wouldn't have given up on her own faith so easily. Perhaps all their lives would be different.

Ben briefly allowed himself to picture an alternate reality where Stephen was alive, his parents were still happily married, and he was the proud holder of a college degree. But that reality didn't include Summer, a thought which made him feel a deep sense of loss. Normally he'd give anything to change the past, to create that different present, but now? The thought of a life without Summer made him feel empty, devoid of any further hope.

In college, there would have undoubtedly been other girls, but would any of them have been the right girl? For that matter, was Summer the right girl, or did she just happen to be the first girl to smile and claim to like him? He didn't know, but now he wanted more than anything to find out.

"Are you ready to go?" he asked with a firm rap on his mother's bedroom door.

When she didn't answer, panic began to set in. Had she drunk herself into a stupor? Was she still sleeping it off? What would Summer think if Ben showed up to the concert all alone?

"Mom?" He twisted the doorknob, but found it locked. He knocked again—louder, harder.

"Hold your horses, hold your horses," Susan answered from within, and then flung the door open.

Ben gasped when he saw his mother standing before him, wearing a dress he'd forgotten she even owned. Her hair was done up in a clean bun, and her complexion looked fresh and even.

"I was putting on mascara, and it's hard to talk with that little wandy thing up close to my eyeball."

"Mom, you look…"

"Good?" She spun to show off the full effect.

"*Gorgeous.* Are you expecting to run into that anchorman at this thing?"

"Haha, very funny. I just wanted to look nice for my future daughter-in-law is all."

"Haha," Ben said sarcastically, but inside his heart swelled. So his mother could see it too.

This thing between him and Summer *was* real.

Summer swung by to pick up Ben and Susan and drive them out to the concert at the nearby church. Even though it wasn't a long drive, she had insisted on escorting them there.

Seeing mother and son emerge from the house dressed a little too formally for an outdoor concert sent warmth coursing through her. Susan looked almost like a different person. She looked healthy, maybe even happy too.

And Ben?

The green polo he wore brought out the flecks of emerald in his eyes. A huge grin crossed his face when he saw her admiring him, and she knew then—beyond the shadow of a doubt—that she had fallen for this small-town boy. Fallen hard.

They had to park in a spare gravel lot a good quarter mile away from the church since all the closer spots were already filled. It seemed all of Sweet Grove had turned up to support the youth group and to enjoy the lively music from the out-of-town bands. As they walked onto the enormous church lawn, a pair of teens greeted them holding donation buckets in their outstretched arms.

"Hi, and thanks for coming! You're the guy from the grocery store, right?" one of them asked, reaching out to shake Ben's hand.

"That's me. Although I normally go by Ben."

"Ben, good to meet you. And who are these two lovely ladies you brought with you today?"

"My mom, Susan, and my… friend, Summer."

"Good, good, the more the merrier. So the concert is free, but we're collecting donations for our upcoming ministry trip to Guatemala. Totally optional, and no pressure. We'll be here the whole time if you decide you want to donate."

Summer took out her wallet and dumped in a twenty.

Ben cleared his throat and looked away.

"Haven't got anything to donate. Otherwise I would," Susan explained. "Hey, perhaps next time you can take up donations for us!"

That was when Elise and Jennifer descended upon them. "Summer, you made it!" Jennifer shouted from across the way, then ran up for a hug.

"And you weren't kidding about bringing a friend," Elise said. "Hi, Susan. Hi, Ben. It's so good to see you both out and about. Maisie will be thrilled you're here. *I'm* thrilled you're here."

Summer watched for any sparks between Elise and Ben, but thankfully those seemed to have died out long ago. Anyway, why was she so jealous? This was ridiculous. They'd dated practically a million years ago. Summer would never go back and date any of her old high school boyfriends, so why did she expect that something would still be lingering between these two?

"Thanks for having us. It's good to get out of the house in the light of day," Susan said, accepting a hug from Jennifer.

"You are always welcome. In fact, I hope we do see you more. You are still my favorite teacher of all time, Mrs. Davis. I went into teaching because of you, you know."

"That's nice, dear," Susan said, in a way that made her seem much older than she actually was.

"Anyway, we won't keep you any longer," Elise said with a wave. "Go enjoy the concert! That's what you came for, right?"

"Yes, indeed," Susan crowed. "See you later!"

Ben whispered apologies, then followed Susan as she set off toward the stage that had been erected on the spacious back lawn of the church. As Susan walked through the crowd, she swung her hips, bobbed her head, and just generally came to life.

Summer glanced toward the stage where a hunky group of twenty-somethings were banging on their instruments in what could only be described as Church Metal. Seemed there was an audience for everything these days. Apparently she'd stopped walking as she watched the band move into a drum solo, because Ben turned around and said something to her. Whatever it was didn't reach her ears; the band was just too loud.

He grabbed her hand and gave it a tug to get her moving once again. Her pulse pounded with even more energy and life than the noisy musicians. Tingles—literal tingles—shot up her arm and warmed her whole body.

She followed him as he followed Susan, and finally they found a place right at the very front of the audience. How long would he hold her hand this time?

"Thank you, Sweet Grove!" yelled the lead singer into the mic, and everyone around them started clapping.

Summer rolled her eyes and joined the wave of applause. So much for *that* question.

Everything was quiet for a few minutes as the next band shuffled onto the stage.

"Look," Ben said, pointing to the far side of the lawn. "There's Maisie."

She followed Ben's long, muscular arm, and sure enough Maisie jumped up and down, waving at them enthusiastically.

"Oh, and Kristina too!" Summer said, spotting her other new friend across the way. "But who are those guys with them?"

"Those guys are Maisie's brothers, Jack, Jonas, and Jared Bryant," Ben patiently explained. The Bryants are kind of the power family of Sweet Grove. Their dad is mayor, and they all own various business in town. The one right next to Kristina is Jeffrey. They work at the diner together. Speaking of which…"

The new guitarist played a few opening chords, and Summer found that she liked their soft rock sound much more than she'd cared for the previous band's performance. She turned her attention back toward the stage, but apparently Ben hadn't finished what he wanted to say.

"Kristina Rose and Jeffrey both work at the diner."

"Yeah?"

"Mabel's on Maple."

"Oh, that's a cute name."

"It's a nice place. Maybe we could go some time."

"Maybe."

"Like on a date."

Oh.

Chapter 11

He'd done it. He'd actually asked Summer out on an official date. This was the beginning of something beautiful…

Except, wait, Summer's petite features pinched into a frown. That wasn't supposed to happen.

Oh, no. Oh, no. Did I misread everything? I really am stupid. Why did I think I deserved someone like her? She's so clearly out of my league, and I'm so obviously kidding myself.

Summer took a deep breath as if she were about to launch into a lengthy explanation of why she had to decline Ben's invitation—and she would have to yell to be heard over the band who had now reached full crescendo. All of Sweet Grove would have a front row ticket to his rejection. *Awesome.*

"Forget it," he said, cutting her off before she could even begin. The last thing he needed was to hear what was coming next. It hurt enough knowing that his dream girl would remain just that—*a dream*, a fantasy.

"No, it's not like that," Summer said, putting a hand on his shoulder and forcing him to look at her. He wasn't the only one looking at her either. Susan watched with a frown that more than likely reflected Ben's own.

"It's okay," he answered, meeting her gaze and hoping his sad eyes wouldn't give him away. Why couldn't he just take it in stride, be a man?

"Ben, I really like you."

"I know," he said between gritted teeth. "We established that last night. You like me, just not enough to say yes, right? It's fine. I shouldn't have asked."

"No, I'm glad you asked. And I do want to spend time with you, Ben. Really." Her voice became uncharacteristically high-pitched. Oh, great. He'd really upset her. "But I'm only here for another couple months. It wouldn't be smart to start something romantic. You get that, don't you?"

He shrugged and tried—but failed—to force a smile onto his pathetic face.

"If it were any other way, I'd love—look at me, Ben—I'd *love* to go on a date with you. But since it's not, let's just be friends. And, no, I'm not blowing you off. I really do want to be your friend. Can we do something together tomorrow? Just maybe not something so… date-y?"

"Does that mean my mom has to tag along again?"

She laughed. "No, let's do something just us."

"And you're sure you want to?"

"Ben, if you don't ask me out again right now, I'm going to ask you."

He put a finger to his lips to keep from speaking, and Summer giggled.

"Oh, so that's how you want to play it? Fine." She took his hand in hers and gave it a squeeze. "Ben Davis, will you please, *please* be my friend?"

"Hmm." He pretended to think about it. "Well, if you insist, then okay."

"And will you go out with me to do something fun tomorrow?"

"I suppose I could be persuaded."

She gave an impatient grunt.

"Yes, I mean *yes*."

"Good, then it's a date."

He quirked an eyebrow.

"A friend date."

"A friend date," he agreed. At least a friend date

was better than no date. After all, how hard could getting out of the friend zone really be?

Friends, buddies, pals, chums, amigos... Perhaps if Summer found the perfect word to describe her relationship with Ben, she would finally stop questioning it. But nothing felt quite right, except for whenever she was around Ben. That felt... perfect.

Comrades, allies, acquaintances, mates... She thought that last one with an Australian accent and smiled to herself.

She was doing a lot of that lately—smiling. Not as if she wasn't a naturally happy person, but lately she was excessively happy, like a clown dancing at the circus level happy. *Mates*, now that wouldn't be so bad.

No! Bad Summer. You're just friends. Friends! And friends don't hurt friends, right?

"Right," she said aloud, wondering if maybe she was just a little touched in the head for answering her own thoughts. Sunny Sunshine squawked from atop his cage, and Summer wondered whether he meant to agree or disagree with her.

"Hey, Sunny. Who's a good bird?" she asked, grabbing a chunk of dried papaya from his treat jar and handing it over to him. She still half-expected him to bite her every time she drew near, but today he just squawked his thanks, transferred the tiny bit of fruit to his foot, and chowed down.

"Good bird," she said, risking a quick stroke on his head. He quacked again, and Summer decided she'd pressed her luck enough for that day.

She returned to the bathroom, spritzed a bit of perfume behind each ear, then wandered over to the kitchen to make herself a cup of tea. Her late night tea date with Ben—a *friend* tea date, obviously—had awakened something in her. Whether she actually relished in the taste or she just liked the memories that were now associated with the hot brew, she couldn't really say for sure.

They'd sat together right here at this very table, said they liked each other. And he'd asked why. She didn't know then, but now she did. How she wished she could go back in time to relive that moment and give him a proper answer.

Ben, I like you because I can tell you do everything with your whole heart, even though I bet you think you don't. You put your own needs on hold to be there for your mom. You helped me before you even knew who I was, and that shows me that you're a good man with a kind heart. This world needs more kindness, Ben, and it's like you have an unending supply. That's why I like you so much, and your awesome good looks certainly don't hurt.

Companions, chums... No, she'd already thought that one, and companions sounded way too intimate, but it also kind of sounded right. Oh, was it getting hot in here? Summer returned to the living room and cracked the window that overlooked the front yard. A nice breeze wafted in, and Sunny Sunshine made a cute little trilling noise.

"That's better now, isn't it, Mr. Bird?" She still felt ridiculous calling the thing Sunny Sunshine. Mr. Bird was perhaps a touch too formal though.

"What's better?" Ben asked from outside.

Her eyes shot up and the first thing she saw were his exposed calf muscles. Beefy, she thought, and then immediately felt like a pervert. There was more to Ben than his gorgeous, gorgeous legs. Like his smile or his straight, white teeth, or...

Chums, chums, chums, she reminded herself.

"Let's go," she said, grabbing her purse from the hook by the front door and joining Ben for their first official friend date.

Chapter 12

"Welcome to Bryant Park Cider Mill," Ben announced as he and Summer pulled into the old dusty drive. He wished he had a car of his own, so that she wouldn't always have to be the one driving them everywhere. Kind of hard to surprise someone when you had to give them step-by-step directions on where to go.

None of this seemed to faze Summer, whose eyes were wide with excitement. "Oh my gosh, I haven't been to the Cider Mill since forever ago. I love it!" And there was that word again—*love*—she loved this, she loved that, but could she learn to love him? Could he convince her that their bond was already far too special to constrain?

"Well, c'mon," he said as they got out of the car. "Let me show you around." He held out his hand to Summer, who took it without hesitation. As they walked she swung their arms back and forth as if they were here as elementary school classmates on a field trip.

They walked into the small shop attached to the mill, which got just enough traffic from out-of-towners and tourists to stay open year round. The scents of cinnamon, caramel, and of course apples swirled in the air. The low lighting seemed to give everything a golden glow, including Summer's cheeks and her curls.

"How's business, Jack?" Ben asked Maisie's eldest brother as he came out from the kitchen to greet them.

"Same as always. How you doing, Ben? Maisie tells me you've been a bit…" His eyes fell to Summer, and he gave her a welcoming smile rather than continuing what he had planned to say.

"Howdy do?" He extended a strong hand toward Summer, and they shook. "You're Iris's niece. Right?"

"Right as rain." Summer giggled. "I don't even know why I said that. I've never used that expression before."

"Seems maybe the Texas is wearing off on you a bit," Jack said and the corners of his eyes pinched from the size of his thousand-watt smile. "Hey, I'm just about to pull a batch of turnovers from the oven. Want one?"

"Yeah, that would be great," Ben said. "Thanks, man."

"I was asking your lady friend," Jack responded with a laugh. "But I suppose I could spare one for you too. So long as you promise to take her over to the old wishing well once you're through."

"Oh my gosh," Summer gasped. "A real, honest-to-goodness wishing well? Ben, we have to go!"

"There's that Texas again," Jack called over his shoulder as he returned to the kitchen. "Are you sure you're not from these parts?"

"If I am, that's news to me," Summer answered, and a second later Jack returned with two awesome-smelling turnovers held in crinkly wax paper.

"For the road," Jack explained.

"Let's eat them on the way to the wishing well." Summer raced out the door despite not knowing where they were going.

"She's real nice, Ben. Don't mess it up," Jack said, tossing a wink his way.

"Believe me, I'm doing my best to not let that happen."

"Ben, c'mon! The wishing well, let's go!" Summer called from a surprisingly far off distance.

He had to jog to catch up with her, and from there it wasn't too much farther to the old well that sat on top of the highest hill in the park.

"Do you have some pennies?" she asked Ben.

"I have dimes, I think. Hang on." He dug around in his pocket and pulled out a small pair of shining coins.

"Ooh, that'll make our wishes ten times more likely to come true. Good thinking!"

Summer closed her eyes and moved her lips in a silent wish, then tossed her coin into the dark depths of the little stone well. "Now it's your turn," she said.

Ben didn't have to think twice about what he wanted to wish for. He smiled at his dream girl, then flipped the coin straight into the well right after hers. The last time he'd made a wish—or rather said a prayer—it had come true. Could he really be so lucky a second time?

At least now he knew that if there really were a God, the dude actually liked him. He added a silent prayer to his wish for extra measure, then grabbed Summer's hands again and took her to explore the beautiful nature trails of the park.

She'd wished for clarity and left it at that. The one word was her whole wish, because there was so much she needed clarity about in her life—her feelings for Ben, her career path, where she should live, her future, everything. She'd listened as that tiny dime ricocheted off the dank stone walls of the well and landed in the water below with a satisfying thunk. Throwing that dime had felt kind of like tossing aside her worries, like she'd entrusted her fate to the old well and that was that. It was the well's problem now, which meant she could just focus on enjoying the rest of that beautiful afternoon with Ben—who may have been a friend, may have been more—only the well could decide now.

As far as what Summer herself wanted, well, the more time she spent with Ben, the more she longed to press herself up against his strong chest and just stay there. Possibly forever. She'd half expected their friend date to end with a sweet, chaste kiss on her doorstep, but Ben had resisted the urge—provided he still had it.

Now that Summer was at home alone again, she drifted dreamily through the house as she got ready for a night in. She'd pop some kernels in her aunt's old fashioned Stir Crazy, open up a bottle of vino, put on her favorite flannel jammies, and Netflix her way into a cheery oblivion. Oh, tonight was going to rock.

Her cell phone began playing the Twilight Zone theme, which was her special ringtone for Aunt Iris— because, let's face it, the woman was a bit out there, and Summer loved that about her.

"Hi, Aunt Iris," she said, clicking over the call to speaker. "How's the cruise?"

"Hi, Summer!" her aunt screamed into the phone. "Can you hear me all right?"

"Uhh, yeah, I think I just popped an eardrum. Take it down a notch or two, and tell me everything." Summer laughed as she situated herself cross-legged on the couch.

"We're at our first big port, and it is absolutely stunning here! It was worth every penny I saved to get here. The salty air, the luxurious dining room, the tropical paradise, it's enough to make an old broad go all moony."

Moony? Where did Iris get her vocabulary words? Still, Summer was beyond thrilled that her aunt's dream had finally become a glorious reality. Iris sounded happier than she'd ever been.

"It sounds fantastic, and you sound so happy," Summer exclaimed. "Have you made any friends?"

"Oh, yes. Everyone is so nice. There's this one gentleman in particular—"

"Ooh, Aunt Iris, you're so bad! Tell me everything. Immediately please."

"I will, but first, how is my little baby?" she asked in a goochie-goo voice. "How's my Sunny Sunshine?"

"She's doing great. She's just…" Summer glanced over toward the large cage in the corner of the room—the cage which now hung open!

Sunny Sunshine was nowhere in sight.

"She's a real character. We…" Summer continued to jabber on as she moved furniture and paced around the house in search of the little yellow bird. That was when she remembered the window—the window directly across from the bird's cage, which she had left wide open before heading off with Ben that afternoon. And that had been hours again. Shoot!

"I-I-I've gotta go, Aunt Iris. Sunny Sunshine sends kisses, and so do I. Call me later, okay? Bye." She rushed to hang up the phone before the tremor in her voice could give her away. Had she really just lost her aunt's favorite companion and best friend?

Oh no, what was she going to do?

Chapter 13

After their lively afternoon at the orchard, Ben came home to find his mother sitting on the couch, one empty liquor bottle on the coffee table before her and another clutched in her hand.

Oh, no.

"Mom?" he asked, craning his neck in an effort to make out her face.

Susan looked up at him with glassy eyes and smiled. Her favorite news anchor droned on in the background. She probably recorded all his segments to watch on loop, Ben realized.

"F-f-finally," she stuttered. "Where have you been all day?"

This is the worst she's been in a while.

"I took the day off work and went to the cider mill with Summer."

"But you never take the day off." She laughed to herself even though the words came out flat.

"Well, I did this time." He sighed and sank onto the couch beside her. Didn't seem he'd be getting away easily until she said whatever she had on her mind. He just hoped her thoughts were coherent enough to follow. If he failed to understand, her frustration would come out in huge spurts. Sometimes, if she got confused enough, she'd even start hitting herself in the forehead, as if somehow the self-harm would shake up her thoughts and rearrange them more logically.

"With Summer, you say?" She stared straight ahead as the news anchor bantered with his female counterpart. Her lips twitched, but she neither smiled nor frowned.

"Yup." *Should I just turn the TV off? Should I try to get her out of the house? Convince her to go to bed?* Ben watched his mother for a few beats in an attempt to better assess her mood.

"I like that girl," Susan said, then let out a big, unapologetic yawn. Bed, she definitely needed to go to bed.

"Okay, Mom. Let's get you tucked in for the night." He reached for her arm to help her out, but she ripped it away.

"No, I'm not ready for bed. Anyway, I've got something to say." Oh, great. Now she was slurring.

"What, Mom?" He sank onto the coffee table so they were sitting knee to knee.

"Don't make the same mistakes I did," she mumbled.

"Okay, Mom." He rolled his eyes, an involuntary response, but what did it matter? She wasn't anywhere near sober enough to pick up on nonverbal cues.

"Don't let..." The next word was indiscernible even though she spoke it with passion.

"What are you talking about?" Ben sighed. "I think maybe you've had enough for today. C'mon, bedtime."

Now she yelled, but at least her words came out clearly. "No, I'm the parent! I'm the parent! You don't tell me what to do. I tell you what to do, and what I'm telling you now is important, so stop telling me to go to bed, and listen!"

He motioned for her to continue. If he still didn't hear her words correctly, then he'd need to pretend. That was the only way to get her to give in and go to bed where she would at least be safe.

"That girl, Summer, you love her," she said, pausing between each word before saying the next. "Don't mess it up."

Now he understood, but he didn't quite know what to make of his mother giving him life advice. Look at them now. Anyone could see which of them had a better chance at messing things up—messing *anything* up.

"How can I love her? I barely know her, and—hey—what makes you so sure I'm going to mess things up?"

Susan leaned in and looked him straight in the eye. Her breath stank of whiskey. Her chapped lips trembled as she spoke. "Because you're your father's son is why. And you're my son too, which is probably even worse."

"Let's get you to bed, Mom. C'mon." He tried reaching for her again, but she took a wide swing at him.

"I'm not going to bed. *You* need to wake up, Ben. You need to wake up and appreciate what you have before it's gone. You understand that? I should have told Stephen how much I loved him, you know." Now he was confused. Was this about Stephen or Summer? And did his mother even know the answer to that question?"

"Mom…" He spoke slowly in an effort to keep her from getting more riled up. "I highly doubt Summer is going to kill herself."

"No, but someone else could snap her up before you work up the nerve. Don't be that guy, Ben. Don't be a loser." She snorted and took another swig of her drink, then said, "You either finish first or you may as well not even join the race. You understand me?"

"Yes, I hear you, Mom. Now are you ready for bed?"

"Fine, fine." Susan stood on shaky feet and allowed Ben to escort her to the bedroom. He filled a tumbler with ice water and set it on her nightstand, then tucked her in. Who was the parent here, again? Ben couldn't even remember the last time he'd had the luxury of innocence, of knowing someone was out there to protect him, to look out for his best interests.

No, that job had been up to him for a long time. It was his job to keep them safe. The only thing he couldn't protect them from was themselves, the demons they invited into their minds and never asked to leave. He and his mom—and even Stephen—were alike in that way. They carried their skeletons in their hearts rather than their closets.

Ben locked up the house, closed all the windows, turned off all the lights. Even though it was still only early evening, apparently bed time had come to the Davis house. Now to decide whether he'd spend the next several hours with Netflix or a book, because he knew he wouldn't be getting any sleep for hours.

He tried reading the volume he had checked out on Jungian psychology, but all the talk of ego bored him to tears. He didn't want to contemplate his unconscious mind and the effect it had on his personal identity. No, he'd much rather think of the beautiful woman he'd spent his afternoon with. Summer made him happy, and she was the only one who had managed to do that in a very long time.

Actually, now that he thought about it, Summer really was the perfect name for her. What was that old sonnet? *Shall I compare thee to a summer's day?* He forgot how it went, but he could practically write the poem himself just thinking of her smile.

Like a summer's day, you are warm with a soft breeze that runs over your skin every so often to perk you up. You are bright, sunny, and you feel like you could be endless. But summer is just one season; it's not meant to last. Maybe that's what makes it so special. But, Summer, I want you all year round. I don't ever want to say good-bye.

Crap, his mother was right. He needed to act on his feelings before it was too late. He couldn't just let the seasons change, couldn't allow his dream girl to move on to whatever came next while he remained behind, feeling the sting of her absence every single day. He needed to talk with her—openly, honestly—and without snapping at her as he'd done before.

He checked in on his mother one last time before changing into his running shoes and taking the trek to Summer's bungalow. Now that he finally had the courage to tell her how he felt without shrinking away at the first sign of discouragement, well, he didn't want to wait another second more than he had to.

He'd been on the track team for the first couple years of high school, but quit after the whole thing with Stephen had gone down. Running to Summer's, he focused on each footfall, on the intensity of his pulse, on the feel of the air he sucked into his lungs with each breath. He would speak from the heart, no rehearsing. Luckily, he'd somehow managed to maintain his winning lung capacity, and he reached Summer's house in record time, leaving no time to second-guess himself.

But when he arrived, he found a small crowd gathered outside the home he'd left only an hour before when they'd said good-bye. What the heck…? This wasn't a party. Everyone looked worried, upset. Where was Summer, and was she okay? His pulse raced, but not from the run.

He spotted his old buddy, Jeffrey, standing at the edge of the swarming pack, next to the garden gnome wearing swim trunks and an inner tube.

"Jeffrey," he called, rushing over. "What's going on? Is everything okay?"

"Hey, man. Good to see you. How long has it been?" Jeffrey's face exploded in a smile, but Jeffrey always smiled about everything. He could probably deliver the worst news in the world and still grin the whole time. Oh, no. Is that what he was doing now?

"Jeffrey, I see you every week when I make the delivery to your diner. Tell me, what's happening here."

"Yeah, but never outside of that, you know? We used to actually hang. Do you remember that?"

"Yeah, yeah, sorry. But it's not time for a history lesson right now, Jeffrey." There's a phrase he never thought he'd say, given that he wanted more than anything—well, almost—to be a history teacher one day. "Tell me what happened," he demanded.

"Oh, I did see you hanging out with that girl at the concert. Summer, right? She seems really nice. I'm happy for you, man."

Ben was about to yell again, but Jeffrey shook his head and finally explained the scene.

"The little bird, Sunny Sunshine, he escaped through an open window or something. Now he's flying all around the neighborhood, hopping between the rooftops and the trees. We think he wants to come down, but he doesn't know how to land or something like that. He's screeching and seems scared. We're all here trying to help, but it doesn't seem to be doing much good." He finished the story and stood smiling, waiting for Ben to say something more.

Ben was less afraid now, but still didn't want to waste time on idle chitchat when Summer needed his help. She must be so upset!

He glanced around and noticed the abundance of ladders—at least six of them by his quick count. One of them was propped up against the side of the house, and Summer was up on the roof waving her arms and trying to attract the bird's attention.

"Oh, hey, Ben!" Sally smiled and waved as his gaze fell on her.

When he waved back, she rushed over to where he and Jeffrey were standing.

"Good to see you, Ben," she said, wrapping him into a hug, which caught him off guard. "Hi, Jeffrey. It's quite an event we have here, isn't it?"

"You said it." Jeffrey agreed by bobbing his head.

"This is one of the biggest gatherings our town has had in years. How much you wanna bet that it will become an annual event now?"

Jeffrey laughed at that idea. Sally did too.

"We'll be celebrating the anniversary of the time Sunny Sunshine escaped for years past anyone even remembers who Sunny Sunshine was."

Haha, very funny. But Ben didn't want to make small talk; he wanted to rescue Summer. Seeing her up on that roof worried him to no end. *What if she falls? Then what?*

"Bye, guys," he mumbled, then ran toward the house, toward Summer.

A wind picked up, and Summer half expected it would blow the tiny parrot straight to Bermuda or wherever it was her aunt's cruise had drifted off to. But strong, little Sunny Sunshine continued to circle overhead, desperately seeking a way to land. Summer followed him with her eyes as he continued to bob from roof to roof, branch to branch, but never to the ground and never to *her* roof where she stood waiting to rescue the danged thing.

The crowd below had grown to a ridiculous size, and new ladders were still being brought over. *Can't you see I only need the one?* She immediately felt bad for thinking it. Her new neighbors only wanted to help. And in a small town like Sweet Grove, an escaped sun conure was big news, apparently—which meant someone was bound to tell her Aunt Iris what had happened. Uh-oh. Hopefully Iris would still be on a high from that cruise by the time she heard the crazy tale that definitely painted Summer as its villain.

The bird took another lap through the sky and even attempted to dive at Summer, but lost his nerve last minute and swooped back up. She followed the orange blur as he landed in a tree at the end of the block. *Great. Just awesome.*

Wait, who's that over there? The crowd began to part like Moses and his sea. A figure emerged in the center, running toward Summer as if his life depended on it.

Ben!

Once again he had come to rescue her. It didn't matter that half the town had also shown up, because somehow *he* had known she needed him and appeared at just the right moment. Yet another sign they were meant to be?

"Ben! Ben!" she shouted, waving her arms even more fiercely than before.

The look on his face was one of pure terror. He ran toward her, pushing others aside in his effort to get to her as quickly as possible. "Come down. Right now!" he said, gripping the base of the ladder so hard his knuckles turned white.

"Aww, Ben, I wasn't going to fall," she argued but complied anyway. Would he find it funny if she pretended to lose her balance and fall? Mmm, probably not. His concern was touching, really. It gave her happy, warm fuzzies.

As soon as her feet landed on the springy front lawn again, she leaped into Ben's arms and wrapped him in a hug. Tears threatened to spill. The jovial, pranky mood she'd had just seconds before completely vanished.

Aww, who was she kidding?

She cried buckets, finally letting everything out now that her savior had arrived.

"Ben, I left the window open and Sunny Sunshine escaped. He's never been outside before. He doesn't know how to come back down. He's scared and upset and apparently stress can kill birds, and I'm so, so worried. I don't know what to do," she said it all in one long breath, then gasped for air and cried some more.

"Keep both feet on the ground for starters. You had me worried." Ben raised his hands and cupped both of her cheeks, then used his thumbs to wipe away a fresh storm of tears. "It's going to be okay."

She wondered for an instant if he was going to kiss her, but then her panic over Sunny Sunshine took center stage once again. "If anything happens to that bird, my Aunt Iris will die. She'll just stop living, Ben. We have to get him back!"

"I'm going up," he said, pushing his sleeves up to the elbows and gritting his teeth as he placed his hands on either side of the ladder.

"I don't think so, young man." Now the cops were here, or at least one of them, and he grabbed Ben by the shoulder.

"Sheriff Grant, the bird, he—"

"I know all about what happened, son, but if anything happens to you, your mother will kill me. *I'll* go get the little fellow. You wait here. Keep her calm." He gestured at Summer, then, before anyone could say a word, the sheriff ascended the ladder and climbed to the peak of the roof.

"Does Sweet Grove really have so little crime that the sheriff personally rescues every animal in need?" she asked in disbelief.

Ben shrugged. "He's the chief of the volunteer fire department too, and as far as Sweet Grove goes, this is exciting stuff. Dramatic stuff," he explained.

In an embarrassingly short amount of time, Sheriff Grant had lured Sunny Sunshine into his outstretched hands and was climbing down the ladder with the bird sitting happily on his shoulder. "Here you go, Miss Smith," he said, handing the creature to Summer.

Summer was so happy she kissed the little bird right on its fluffy head. Sunny Sunshine screamed at her, but did not bite. Still, he clearly knew whose fault all of this had been.

"How's your mother doing, son?" Summer heard Grant ask as she rushed inside to return the bird to its cage. If she pushed her luck too much, he would definitely bite her and she would toss the thing so hard he'd need to be rescued again.

When Summer came back into the yard, the crowd had already begun to dissipate.

"We're all heading to Mabel's on Maple to celebrate," Ben explained. "C'mon!"

Chapter 14

The crowd shuffled into Mabel's diner, half of its off-shift employees in tow.

"Table for twenty-seven," Jeffrey called toward the back kitchen, then took it upon himself to start pushing tables together in the center of the dining room floor.

"I know that was a near tragedy and all," he said to Ben, plopping into the chair beside him, "but it was also the most fun I've had in weeks."

Ben laughed and gave Jeffrey the thumbs up while scanning the group for Summer. The chair to his right was still open, and he wanted to make sure she got it. When at last he spied her standing and chatting with Maisie and the other women, he waved her over.

But, unfortunately, Sally thought he was waving at her. She rushed right over, sat down gingerly beside Ben, then crossed her legs at the knee.

"I'm not sure I've ever seen you outside the library," she said without preamble.

"I have," Jeff said, leaning forward to talk to Sally through Jeff. "Just the other day I saw him at the church concert. We missed you there by the way, Sally."

Sally tilted her head to the side like an inquisitive husky puppy. "Did you now?" She broke out into a large, self-assured smile. "Well, I might have gone had I known Ben would be there."

"Yup, yup, he was." Jeffrey bobbed his head as he spoke. "You came with your mom and with Summer, right?"

"With Summer?" Sally asked, whipping her head back with a snort.

Ben and Jeffrey both stopped talking and stared at Sally who seemed to be working something out inside her head.

"I remember now," she said with a triumphant look. "I saw you two talking in the library the other day. Are…? Are you two an item?"

Ben's face felt like it was on fire. He glanced around again for Summer, hoping that just looking at her would give him the right answer. Because honestly he didn't know whether they were an item or an *almost*-item. They'd certainly become more than friends, but until he knew how to define their relationship, it didn't feel right to label it for others.

He found Summer sitting with Kristina Rose clear at the other end of the table. Their eyes met and she winked at him.

He grinned back at her, which apparently was more than enough to answer Sally's question.

"Oh, I see," she said, accepting a glass of water from Mabel herself who had come over to wait on the large group.

"Of course you bring in all this business on your day off, Jeff," the old woman joked, then filled his glass too.

"We're celebrating, Mabel. Join us!"

Mabel clicked her tongue. "And if I do that who will wait on you? Next time, my friends, next time."

Mabel scuttled back toward the kitchen, and Sally excused herself to go to the restroom.

This was his chance! If he invited Summer to take Sally's seat for herself, would that be rude? Would it matter? It had started to feel as if Sally needed a strong, clear signal that he was interested in someone else. The funny thing was if she had shown even a glimmer of interest in him less than two weeks ago, he'd have happily started a romance with her instead.

But now that he'd met his real, honest-to-goodness dream girl, all bets were off and all chances were nonexistent for a certain cheeky librarian.

He stood and took bold, confident steps in Summer's direction. That was when his phone started buzzing wildly at his hip. He groaned and fished the old-fashioned flip phone out of his pocket. *MOM* flashed across the screen in green and black.

So much for grabbing his chance while he could...

When he picked up the phone he could barely hear his mother over the din of the noisy diner, but her words came out a jumbled mess anyway.

"Ben! He's... and I... but we..." Susan heaved between giant, racking sobs.

"Can you hear me? Hang tight, Mom. I'm coming home."

He shot one last glance toward Summer, took a deep breath, then headed away from what he hoped would not be his last chance at this particular dream come true.

A blur of movement caught Summer's attention. She'd already been watching him from the corner of her eye, and now she turned to take in the full sight of Ben as he strode toward her. *He's coming over. This is it. Are we going to hold hands again? Are we finally going to kiss tonight?*

Her thoughts zoomed, but not once did she wonder whether this was what she really wanted, *who* she really wanted. She was all in for Ben, only...

She had told him they needed to stay just friends. Her stupid big mouth! Ben seemed too much a gentleman to deliberately go against her wishes. Did that mean she'd have to make the first move this time?

Ben frowned, drew out his phone, stopped walking. She saw him mouth a string of words; the only one she could discern was *Mom.* He frowned again, deeper this time.

Susan, Susan, what are you doing? Summer's brain shouted. *I thought we were friends! C'mon, Susan...*

She should have jumped up to join Ben as he hurried out of the busy diner, but by the time she came to this realization, he had already left and Maisie had jumped deep into a discussion of the time she and Kristina Rose had snuck into the rival school after hours to steal their team mascot's costume. Those crazy girls—the more she learned about them, the more she adored them.

She listened to the story, laughed in all the right places and tried not to think of Ben.

But then a girl she recognized as the librarian came up behind her and placed an icy hand on Summer's shoulder.

"Can I talk to you?"

Summer gulped but ventured a nod.

"Come over here," the girl said, leading her to one of the empty booths by the window. "So you like Ben," she said once they'd both seated themselves.

Well, that was unexpected and, to be honest, pretty rude. Summer took a moment to collect herself before answering, but even then she couldn't fully hide her disgust. "Umm, excuse me? Why would you say that? I don't even know your name, yet somehow you think—"

"I'm Sally," the other girl interrupted. "You're Summer, right?" She stared at Summer with steel gray eyes that looked like ice against her snowy complexion. She'd be a real-life Elsa of Arendelle if not for her jet black hair and the absence of that fabulous gown.

Summer glanced back at her friends who were watching this conversation with confused expressions, then nodded. Perhaps if she gave the girl what she wanted this would all be over quicker?

"And you like Ben," Sally said flatly.

Summer hesitated, but then nodded again. "Am I really that obvious?" she squeaked.

"Yes, yes, you are. But so is he."

Summer drummed her fingers on the table. What was she supposed to say now? This whole thing was terribly uncomfortable, but the other woman either didn't notice or didn't care.

"When did you move to town?" Sally pressed.

"About a week ago, I guess. I'm watching my Aunt Iris's shop while she... Why are you asking me so many questions? It's weird."

"I figured as much."

"Umm..." Figured what? Weren't librarians supposed to be good with their words, or was all that time spent quietly among books bad for their social skills?

Sally sighed as if somehow she knew exactly what Summer was thinking—knew and strongly disapproved. "Ben's been sad for years. Then about a week or so ago, that seems to have started to change. Which is why I *figured* that was about the time you came into the picture."

"I met Ben about a week ago," Summer confirmed.

"Yeah, like I said, I figured *that part* out." She sighed again. "As much as I hate to say it, you seem to be good for him."

"Thanks?"

"It's *you* who should be thankful. He's a great guy."

"What's your name again?"

"Sally." She frowned as if Summer had been the one to corner her and not the other way around.

"It sounds like you like Ben too, Sally," Summer said, then stood up to take her leave.

Sally grabbed her wrist before she could walk away. "If you hurt him, no one in this town will ever forgive you."

Hurt him? Why would she hurt him? Of course, she only wanted the best for Ben, but she didn't owe this Sally girl any explanations. She shrugged off the weirdness of their conversation and headed back over to her real friends. Now she wanted Ben more than ever before. Nobody told her who or what she could or couldn't have. And it seemed if she didn't date Ben herself then this psycho would try to move in and claim him.

She wanted Ben—needed Ben—and it seemed like he needed her too. Now they just had to get past all their flirtations and finally start something real.

She was ready.

Chapter 15

When Ben returned home, he found his mother sitting hunched over the kitchen table. Its surface was so cluttered he couldn't even see the wood beneath. Old photo albums, empty liquor bottles, clothes that had belonged to his father that he hadn't realized his mother had saved, all lay together in a giant, scattered heap.

"Ben!" she wailed. "Did you know he got married again?"

Okay, so this breakdown wasn't about Stephen as it usually was, but rather about his deadbeat dad.

"Good for him," Ben said, putting an arm under each of his mother's armpits and pulling her to a fully seated position.

She turned to him, her eyes glassy with tears, her lower lip trembling like that of a child about to throw a tantrum.

"Her name is Megan, and she works at the news."

So that was why she was always watching the nightly news. It had nothing to do with the charming male anchor and everything to do with the *usurping adulteress*—or so said his mother at least—who read the news alongside him.

"She j-j-just had a b-b-baby!" Susan shouted and then fell face forward onto an open photo album spread out in front of her.

"Mom, it's fine. He was no good for us anyway."

"What do you mean? Everything was better when he was still here."

"No, everything was better before that jerk Stephen shot himself and ruined our lives!"

"Ben, how could you…?" Why did she always have to act as if Ben were to blame for her misery? Ben was the only one still holding this family together. He'd given up so much for her, but did she even realize that? Did she even care?

"We're all hurting. Every one of us, and I bet Dad is too," he said through clenched teeth. Here was his mother drudging out their bleak past when he so desperately wanted to focus on the future—a future that just moments ago had seemed so vibrant with possibilities.

"But he has a new life, a pretty wife, a second chance at kids," Susan argued, shaking her head. "Oh, Ben, I've lost everything that ever mattered."

"I'm still here," he whispered. Suddenly he felt too tired to argue.

Susan broke down in a fit of sobs. She lifted one of his father's old flannel shirts to her face and buried her face in the worn fabric. She wouldn't even look at Ben, wouldn't even acknowledge that he was standing right there, where he'd been for the past twenty years.

"I'm still here," he said again, wondering if that even mattered, if it was even true. For the past week, his head and heart had both been with Summer. Clearly he'd neglected his poor mother. Looking at her now was proof of that.

His inner critic returned more hostile than ever. *You don't deserve to be happy, Ben. Look what you did to your poor mother. You make me sick!*

Susan continued to wail in the kitchen, but no matter how loud she got it wasn't enough to drown out the stream of self-hate that flowed to Ben's heart.

You did this to her. You! It's all your fault. Summer deserves better, and you know it!

He'd messed everything up by daring to dream. Hadn't he killed that part of himself long ago? He took a few deep breaths and then brought his mother a beer from the garage. He briefly contemplated grabbing one for himself too, but what good would that do?

Honestly, he'd just rather die.

Oh, and he had been so close to happiness. He was a selfish, foolish man. A jerk. Like Stephen—and like his father.

"I'm going to bed," he told his mother after the sobbing had finally subsided. "Don't stay up too late." He kissed her on the head, then took his leave. He also took a couple sleeping pills. The last thing he needed was a restless night, or worse, a never-ending dream loop reliving his sweet time with Summer.

She'd be gone soon enough, move on to a better life—one she deserved, but he didn't.

He only had to manage to avoid her for another few weeks.

Summer had hoped Ben would stop by Morning Glory's after his shift at the market, but he didn't. She had hoped he'd give her a call or even show up at her doorstep that evening, but he didn't do that either. So she did the only thing she could do—she took matters into her own hands and called *him* rather than waiting around like a helpless damsel.

He didn't answer.

Okay, so maybe she would have to do a little bit of waiting, but she felt confident he'd call back. He would... Wouldn't he?

Well, it had been clear he'd been on his way to talk with her when he got the call that tore him away from their impromptu gathering at Mabel's diner. And he'd showed up at her house again that evening very shortly after they'd ended their friend date... What had he come to say?

And *what* was keeping him away?

Oh, no. Wait a second!

What if something had happened, something so bad he hadn't had a chance to call in the last twenty-four hours? What if he or Susan was hurt and rather than helping she'd moped around all day wondering why he hadn't called? They weren't even dating yet and already she was a terrible girlfriend.

Unless, of course, he was waiting for *her* to make a move. After all, she'd been the one to insist they were better off as friends. Had he taken that to heart? Was he holding back out of respect for what she'd claimed she'd wanted?

She didn't like that idea very much. *Ugh.* Why had she been so insistent? Why couldn't she have left things a little open? She dialed Ben's number again, but still no answer.

Now she was really worried, confused, and every emotion that fell between the two. With all the angst and uncertainty she felt about her future career, she at least knew she wanted *this*, wanted to see where things could go with Ben. So she needed to be bold, needed to pursue what she wanted with unapologetic passion. She needed to stop by his house to make sure everything was all right—to make sure *they* were all right.

Not even the niggling fear of rejection that tickled at the back of her mind could stop her as she fired up her sedan and drove to Ben's neighborhood. This is right, she told herself. He'll be happy to see you.

But when she arrived outside the squat ranch, she found the windows completely dark, the house as still as the night around it. They didn't have a car, so she couldn't check to see whether it was still in the garage and all the curtains were drawn, which meant no peeking through the windows. The last thing she wanted to do was disturb Susan if she'd finally managed to get some rest.

Hmm…

Perhaps she could try again tomorrow. She had to be worrying herself over nothing, right?

Chapter 16

"What's with you?" Ben's mom mumbled as he shuffled past on his way to the kitchen.

"What?" he muttered back, continuing toward the fridge to grab a cold can of soda.

He took a long swig then turned back toward the door, ready to lose himself in Netflix for the evening once again. Susan's stood in the arched doorway, her bony frame a living shadow as she pressed a hand up against each side.

He stepped to the side and waited for her to pass, but she kept stock still. Only her eyes flitted back and forth as if assessing him.

"What's with you?" she asked again.

He shrugged, trying to hide just how much he didn't want to deal with her at the moment. "Nothing," he said. "Will you please move?"

But he knew that whenever his mother got something stuck in her mind, she refused to drop it without a fight. Sure enough, she sighed and asked, "What happened to that nice girl, Summer?"

"She's gone." He took another drink, trying to act cool, as if this fact didn't bother him in the slightest.

"She left town?"

"No, but she may as well have. Will you please move now?"

Susan groaned and stepped aside. Ben had assumed he was off the hook, but no—she followed him into his bedroom and sat down at his swivel desk chair.

"What?" he grumbled. "Can't I have any privacy?"

Susan's hands shook, despite her best attempts to contain them calmly in her lap. "Did you and Summer get in a fight?"

"No."

"Then why are you moping around like the whole world is coming to an end?"

"I don't want to talk about it, okay?"

"Too bad, you're talking." She picked up his legs and laid them on her lap, the way she used to do when he was a little boy and came home sore from soccer practice. She massaged little circles in his calves and waited for him to answer the question she'd already asked half a dozen times.

Was she really going to make him say it? He took a deep breath and did his best to explain it gently. "I decided to stop seeing Summer. My decision. *Me*. There was no fight or anything. It's just not a good time for me is all."

"Why isn't it a good time?"

Neither said anything as the truth of the situation sank in.

Susan's eyes widened and she pushed Ben's legs to the floor. "Oh, I see."

He waited for her to charge out of the room, taking offense as he'd known she would.

But she surprised him once again, this time by choosing to stay. She rose from the desk chair and came to sit beside him on the bed. "Because of me," she said plainly, perhaps the truest thing she'd ever admitted.

He nodded, unable to voice the words even though they were being communicated anyway.

"The other day... You think... You think that my breakdown was because you'd let me down in some way?"

He nodded again.

"No, Ben, no." Her voice became scratchy, meek.

Ben looked up, expecting her to burst into tears, but instead she was smiling and staring straight at him as she spoke.

"I am so happy for you and Summer. It just made me miss what I once had with your father. I know it's awful to be jealous of you, to be jealous of my kid, but we both know I'm not the best person—or the best mother—anyway."

Ben knew he should argue here, but he was tired—*much too tired.*

"I don't regret what I had with your father," she continued."Even when love hurts, it's still worth feeling. Don't take the weight of all my problems onto your shoulders. I've already ruined my own life. The last thing I want is to ruin yours too, okay?"

"I don't need your help to ruin my life, Mom. I'm managing to do it just fine on my own."

"Well, if you change your mind, you know where to find me." She gave him an awkward side hug then left.

Yes, I know where to find you—passed out drunk on the couch.

Sure enough, a few moments later the unmistakable sound of a wine cork popping filled the otherwise silent house. Ben knew then more than ever:

it didn't matter how much he or anyone else wanted them to, some things would never change.

Summer's phone broke her out of a dead sleep. *Buzz, buzz, buzz.*

Who the heck would be calling at this hour? She groped around on her nightstand until she clutched the rude device in her hand, then pressed the button on her touch screen to answer the call. The time only read ten-something and she'd gone to bed more than a couple hours ago. Ben calling.

"Hello?" she answered, doing her best to sound chipper as she smoothed her bedhead. *Wait, this is the phone, he can't see me.*

But the voice that greeted her didn't belong to Ben. "Summer?" said a woman whose voice she couldn't quite place.

Ben's mom. It has to be Ben's mom. Who else would be calling from his phone?

"Yup, it's me. Is this Susan?" She did her best to hide her disappointment, but judging by Susan's reaction it came through crystal clear.

"Yeah."

Summer waited for her to say more, but the line stayed quiet. "Is everything okay?"

Susan sighed. Summer tried to figure out whether her caller had been crying or if she'd just had too much to drink, but it was hard to tell the difference with Susan.

"No," Ben's mother said, then sighed again.

"Oh my gosh! Did something happen to Ben? I'll be right over." Before she could stop them, the most vivid and horrible images filled Summer's head—Ben lying bandaged and broken in a hospital bed, Ben having run away, Ben lying on the side of the road in a ditch somewhere, Ben—no, she couldn't bring herself to think that last one. It was too terrible.

"No, no, it's not like that," Susan assured her.

Summer wished Susan had started the conversation by letting her know everything was all right. Now she felt more than a bit angry at the needless drama. She waited for Susan to explain herself, but she didn't offer more. "Does he know you took his phone?"

"No."

"Did you call me by accident?"

"No, I meant to call." The words were slurred, answering Summer's earlier question. Susan had been drinking—lots, from the sound of it.

"What do you need?" Summer asked impatiently. "I was sleeping, you know."

Susan wailed in response—a full-bellied, anguished cry of pain.

And Summer immediately felt guilty. "Whoa, whoa, it's okay. I'm sorry, I didn't mean—"

"I can't even do this right," Susan sobbed.

"*Do what?* Please tell me what's wrong."

"Everything is wrong. Ben is a good boy. He deserves good things, but he's never gotten them. Because of his brother, because of me."

So this was about something, about Ben. "Yes, I like Ben very much and he does seem to have a... complicated life, but you can't blame yourself for that." Even as she spoke the placating words, she knew it was a lie. Susan probably did as well.

A brief silence fell between them again, but this time Susan pressed forward toward whatever the goal of this conversation was. "You do, though? You really like him?"

Now Summer sighed. "Of course I do. Susan, I'm confused. What's this about? Do you need me to come over?"

Having found her courage, Susan's words now came out quick and enthusiastically. "Will you come out on a date tomorrow night? If I set it up, will you come?"

"You want me to cook dinner again? Sure, I guess I could do that. What time should we—?"

"No, not all of us. Just you and Ben. Will you have dinner with him tomorrow night? A date?"

"At your house, or…?" Summer let the question linger. While she wanted to go out with Ben more than anything, it felt odd to have his mother spring it on both of them as a surprise. He hadn't returned her calls for a reason, after all—whether or not she knew what that reason was.

"No, I'll make a reservation at Ernie's. He doesn't know I called, but I can get him there at six. Will you be waiting?"

"Umm, sure, I guess." Summer was too shocked to disagree. Besides, she really did want to see Ben. She only hoped that he would be happy to see her too and that tomorrow's "date" wouldn't end in complete disaster.

Chapter 17

It had not been a good day for Ben. A group of teenagers had decided it would be funny to trash aisle four, and he'd needed to stay well past quitting time to clean up after them. By the time he reached home—almost an hour later than expected—he just wanted to crawl into bed and sleep his misery off.

Unfortunately, his mother seemed to have a different idea as to how he should spend his evening. She was stuck on him like glue from the moment he stepped in the door. "Hi, Ben. Did you have a good day at work?"

"No. I just want to go straight to bed. Good night."

"No bed for you, young man." She laughed in a way that was uncharacteristic of her—almost giddy.

"Anyway, your awful, no-good, terrible day is about to get a whole lot better. *Here.*" She thrust a freshly ironed shirt into his chest. "Put this on, and wear your good pants. The black ones."

"Mom, I—"

"Hush, not a word. Just get ready. Go, go!" She shoved him toward his room, still way too chipper for his liking.

"But—"

"Nope, go put that on. Then we'll talk." She crossed her arms, and that was that. The issue wasn't up for further argument, apparently.

Ben had always been a good son. He'd honored his mother, respected her—even when she didn't deserve it. So he did what he was told, reminding himself all the while that her being happy was a good thing, something he should fight to preserve, no matter how much she annoyed him.

He fished his *good pants* from the bottom drawer of his old dresser and smoothed them out, then buttoned up the freshly ironed shirt and tucked it into his waist band. *There. Now what?*

Susan gasped and then laughed again as he returned to the hallway where she stood waiting.

"Well, don't you look handsome? You'd do well to dress up more often."

"And why am I dressed up, exactly?" He looked over his mother who was wearing an old bathrobe and flannel pajama pants that didn't quite meet her ankles. "And why aren't you?"

But Susan's train of thought had taken a nostalgic detour. "You look just like your father when we first met, oh!" She suddenly snapped out of it. "But I won't go any further down that road, you hear? Besides you need to get going before you're late!"

"Late? Mom, I don't understand what you're up to, but please, for both our sakes, just stop." He began to undo the top buttons of his shirt, more than ready to replace it with a more comfortable ensemble.

Susan slapped his hands away from his collar. "You should watch how you talk to me. I've done you a favor. Now go to Ernie's. Reservation's at six."

Ernie's just happened to be the most expensive restaurant in town—the only expensive restaurant in town. He'd eaten there once in high school maybe, but as an adult he preferred to spend his hard-earned money on more practical things, like electricity or the mortgage payment. "And how are we supposed to afford this? And, Mom...? Wait, is this about Summer? You didn't!"

His mother shook her head and pressed a crisp one-hundred dollar bill into his hand. "Don't ask, just go."

"Fine, I'll go. But only to apologize. You've gone too far this time. I told you I didn't need your help, and you—"

"Ben?"

"What?"

"Shut up, and go get your girl."

Summer sat waiting at a table for two that overlooked the rolling hills of the cider mill. The pretty cloth that covered the table was embroidered with lace, and everything else about the place felt fancy and old-fashioned too. She watched the people come and go, most of whom she didn't recognize in the slightest—although she thought she spied one of Maisie's brothers across the small, well-kept dining room. Closer by, a middle-aged African American couple clinked champagne glasses together and stared lovingly into each other's eyes.

Would this be her and Ben twenty-odd years from now? Celebrating the anniversary of their first official date at the place that had started it all? She wanted it to be so, but she also had no idea what the next two months would bring, let alone the next two decades. Oh, she needed to figure that out soon.

Hopefully tonight would prove a nice distraction from the looming sense of dread at having to finally choose a path for her life. Hopefully, too, Ben would be glad for his mother's interference and things wouldn't be awkward between them as they shared a gourmet meal. Hopefully, hopefully, hopefully...

All she had these days was hope—hope that she'd make the right decision about her future, hope that she and Ben could find a way to make things work despite it all, hope that her life would end up better than her mother's had.

That was when Ben turned up, right as Summer was compiling her mental list of one hope after another. He'd dressed himself nearly identically to the wait staff in his dark slacks and white, buttoned shirt, but he lacked their confidence and poise. She liked that very much about him, actually—how real he always seemed, how uncorrupted. Summer lifted her arm and waved to him, hoping—yes, *again with the hope*—that the gesture wasn't too uncouth for such a ritzy establishment.

The motion caught his eye and he turned toward Summer then froze, not like a deer in headlights but rather like a man who'd set his eyes on exactly the thing he wanted and now had to pause to take it all in. And in Ben's case that thing was her. No one could mistake the sparkle that played in his eyes for anything but love. *Love, eek!* His eyes said all the word she hadn't been able to bring his lips to speak.

Since he still didn't move, Summer stood and walked over to him instead.

"Fancy meeting you here," he said.

"Fancy is right." She laughed. "Care to join me at our table?"

"I knew I was forgetting something." He laughed too as he held out his arm to her, and together they took their seats. He even pulled out her chair like a proper Southern gentleman.

"You look so beautiful tonight, I almost forgot how furious I am with my mother for going behind my back like this." He smiled, then frowned immediately. "I'm so sorry about that by the way."

"Don't be. I was a bit embarrassed at first, but now I'm just glad to be here together."

"Welcome to Ernie's," the waiter said, having chosen exactly that moment to attend to his new diners. "My name is Tobias. I'll be taking care of you this lovely evening. To start, I have some of our famous Bavarian salt bread for the table. May I interest you in our house Pinot Grigio?"

"No!" Summer and Ben answered in unison, then broke apart in a fit of giggles.

The waiter smiled, but did not join in the laughter. "Very well. I'll be back to take your orders once you've had time to review our specials."

"Do you know him?" Summer asked, spreading homemade butter across her roll.

"Never seen him before in my life."

"But it's a small town and he looks about our age. Wouldn't you have grown up together?"

Ben shook his head. "He probably went to the private school in Garnet Hills. Anyway, I have something a bit more important I'd like to talk about. If that's okay?"

Summer motioned for him to continue as she bit down into her crazy delicious piece of bread. German food. Who knew it could be so divine?

Ben cleared his throat, took a quick drink of water, then continued. "So I have no idea what my mother actually told you, so please could you let me know..." His cheeks flushed as he lowered his eyes toward the table then looked up again. "Is this another friend date, or…?"

She did her best to keep her face neutral. She wouldn't answer his question until he could answer one that had been bothering her these past several days. "Why didn't you call me back?"

"What?" Ben frowned. It transformed his entire face in a way she didn't like, but she also needed to know why he'd avoided her until now.

"We had a good time that day at the Cider Mill. Didn't we? And then after Sunny Sunshine escaped, I thought you'd come back to… But then you didn't call and you didn't return my calls, and I just didn't know if—"

"Summer, stop. I'm sorry."

"You don't have to apologize," she offered. "I just want to know *why*."

"Yes, I do have to apologize. I really am sorry. Disappearing like that wasn't fair of me. I just got worried."

"About?"

"Worried that maybe I like you too much."

"Well, did you ever stop to think that maybe I like you too much too?"

The smile returned to his face once more. He

looked so handsome, so happy in that moment. "So it's *not* a friend date."

She lifted her water goblet and clinked it to his. "To our first *date* date," she toasted. And in that moment, she was glad they'd passed on the wine. Because she knew she'd want to remember this perfect evening for a long time to come.

Chapter 18

Summer had returned, or rather he'd returned to her—and now Ben just couldn't stop smiling. He continued to smile even as his cruel inner critic tried to convince him otherwise.

It would be better if you just left well enough alone. She's got enough going on in her life already, and she doesn't deserve to be saddled with all your problems on top of it.

No, he needed to get out of his head. To stop analyzing every moment and focus on living them instead. There's a beautiful girl here that obviously likes you, he reminded himself, realizing then how much he sounded like his mother—or at least the sober version of her.

And it would be better if—

No. It wouldn't. I was on the brink of taking the same road Stephen took. I asked for a miracle, and now here she is. Ben needed to stop talking to himself and start talking to Summer again.

He reached across the table and took her hand in his. "I'm sorry if I'm being rude," he said. "I just get a little lost in my head sometimes."

She rubbed her thumb in circles over his and smiled at him reassuringly. "Got the angel and devil on your shoulders?"

"I'm not sure I follow..."

"Like in the cartoons," she explained. "The good and bad sitting on your shoulders whispering advice to you."

He laughed at how well she already knew him. "Yeah, something like that."

"Well, I hope they're saying good things about me. If they're not, you better kick their butts into gear and tell them to be nice." She winked at him before taking a slow sip of water from her crystal goblet.

"Actually, they were just suggesting that maybe we should take advantage of having the whole evening laid before us rather than saying good-bye." He looked down at his desert plate scraped clean of the cheesecake that had once sat upon it. Dinner had shot by in a flash. Every moment had felt perfect, even the moments he'd spent arguing with himself in his head. There was no longer any argument against being with Summer. Even his inner critic knew that this was right.

"Are you trying to ask me something, Ben? If so, just ask it. You know I'll say yes." She batted her lashes flirtatiously, and he fell even harder for her in that moment.

"Okay, okay. I… Summer, would you like to accompany me to…um. Shoot."

They both laughed, and she squeezed his hand which still held firmly onto hers. He didn't ever want to let go.

"I guess I didn't think that question all the way through. How about we walk to, to, uhh…"

"C'mon, Ben," she urged kindly. "You're the one who lives here."

"I've got it! How about we go back to the Cider Mill since you enjoyed it so much the last time we were there? Want to?"

"Yes." She stood before he could pull out her chair for her.

Ben dropped the one-hundred dollar bill his mother had given him onto the table without bothering to wait for change.

Luckily, the restaurant overlooked the cider mill's vast and beautiful park, so they didn't have far to walk before they reached their destination. In the distance, moonlight glinted merrily off the dark lake. Did this setting always look so beautiful, or had Ben's entire outlook changed, thanks to the dream of a woman walking beside him?

Whatever the reason, he liked the outcome. He liked feeling happy, hopeful—almost free in a way. And he had a pretty good idea Summer felt the same way just now. Continuing to stare at the horizon as they walked, Ben reached over and felt for her hand.

As her fingers tangled with his, he felt a weight he hadn't even realized he'd been carrying rise into the air and float away. *Now* he was free.

If holding her hand felt this earth-shaking, what would kissing her be like? And did she want it? Would it be too soon? Or…?

Summer's laugh broke through the calm night sky as they found themselves on the familiar path that led to the old park bridge. She held tightly to his hand as she pressed her body against his, almost as if she could read his thoughts, almost as if she knew exactly what he wanted in that moment—as if she wanted it too.

But just as quickly as she'd embraced him, she pulled away. "Race you to the bridge!" she yelled as she began running away from him.

Well, he wasn't going to let her get away that easily. He followed her down the path, his heart absolutely bursting with joy.

If I beat her, he told himself, then I'll kiss her. If I don't, then I will anyway.

Summer made it to the bridge a few paces behind Ben. Although her breaths now came out in short puffs, Ben's breathing remained easy, effortless. "You could have told me you were an Olympic level athlete!" she joked.

"Well, I do have the record at Sweet Grove High for fastest one-hundred-meter dash." She couldn't tell for sure in the darkening sky, but it seemed like he winked at her.

"I haven't got any records like that, so I think I need to sit down now and take a rest." She pushed her legs through the rails of the bridge, allowing her feet to dangle over the water beneath them.

Ben quickly joined her. The heat from his body warmed hers even though they weren't yet touching.

"Are you good at everything you try?" she asked seriously.

"Everything except life itself," he answered, then jumped back to his feet and wandered off the bridge and onto the small beach below. Had she made a mistake? She'd been trying to compliment him, to flirt, but now here she was sitting on her own in the middle of a night that had once seemed so perfect.

She hesitated before deciding that, yes, she should probably go look for him. But before she could clamber fully back to her feet, Ben had returned. He sat back down with her and handed her a small, white flower. "I saw this, and I wanted you to have it. Plus, I needed some time to think of a better answer to your question."

Summer shot him a confused look.

He smiled and rolled his eyes. "You asked if I'm good at everything. It was like two minutes ago. Remember?"

She laughed. "Oh, that. You don't have to—"

"The truth is *I'm not*. Look at my life, Summer. It was a hopeless mess before you turned up. But now, with you, somehow I feel like maybe I can do anything, maybe I'm not such a screw-up, after all."

"Because of me?" she squeaked.

"Because of you. What about you? What are you best at?"

"That's the thing. I'm not really best at anything. I have no idea what I want to do with my life. I'm afraid if I choose one thing, I'll be letting go of everything else, you know?"

He swung his feet back and forth as if running through the night air. "But in not choosing, you hang onto nothing."

"Okay, Confucius. You told me you wanted to be a history teacher. How did you know? Like *really know* that's the one thing you wanted?"

"Well, first off, my mom was a teacher, so it's kind of in my blood. But also I just never wanted to stop learning. I feel like knowledge can take you anywhere even if you never leave your backyard."

"Now you sound like a PBS special." She laughed again. She laughed so much whenever she was with Ben. "I like it. *I like you.* Quite a lot, actually."

"I like you too." He bumped his shoulder into hers and slid a little closer so that now they were sitting hip to hip. "That's why I gave you that flower."

"*That's* why, huh?" She twirled the stem in her hand and watched the white petals spin. "Not to remind me that I'm a crap florist?"

He laughed heartily. "Nope, because it looked so pure and beautiful down by the bank. It reminded me of you, that there daisy."

"Daisy? How do you know it's not an aster?"

"It *is* an aster," he answered with a subtle smirk.

"But you said…?"

"It's an aster *and* a daisy, because a daisy is a type of aster. It's kind of like how a square is also a rectangle, but not every rectangle is a square."

"Huh?" Her head hurt a little now, but she liked that Ben knew the answer even if she didn't quite understand it herself.

He shook his head and let out a slow breath. "Sorry, I get a little…"

"Teachery?" she supplied.

He grinned.

"It really *is* in your blood. You have it all figured out."

Ben scoffed. His previously playful tone turned serious. "Hardly. I know what I want but not how to get it. I'm so afraid that if I pursue my own dreams I'll let everyone down. My mom, Maisie, and even Stephen's memory. Pretty ridiculous, huh?"

"Not at all. I get where you're coming from. I've always been afraid of taking that leap of faith too. I've worried that…"

"You wouldn't like where you landed?"

She touched her nose to let him know his guess

was exactly right. When she lowered her hand back to her lap, he took it in both of his.

His green eyes focused on her without blinking. "What are you so afraid of?" he asked.

"Making the wrong choice," she admitted, giving his hand a squeeze. Could they maybe change the subject and talk about happier things now?

Ben, though, seemed determine to pursue the issue. "But in making no choice, you instead—"

"I know," she said, and it was true. She understood all her limitations, but what she didn't understand is what had gotten in the way for Ben all these years, why he hadn't fought for himself. So she asked, "What are *you* so afraid of?"

He looked up at the sky as if to draw strength, and answered her while staring at the stars. "Never amounting to anything," he confessed. "Killing myself when it all becomes too much."

Well, she had not expected to hear that. Especially since Ben knew firsthand how much a decision like that could hurt those who had been left behind. She gasped. "You wouldn't!"

He turned back toward her, his face looked pale, whether from the moonlight or from the weight of his words, she couldn't be certain. "I very nearly did."

What do I say to that? I'm glad you didn't kill yourself? Thanks for sticking around?

Ben continued, relieving her of having to find a response. "The day we met, actually."

She thought back to that day. Ben's coldness slowly giving way to warmth, him saying he had somewhere he needed to be but then sticking by her side for hours. "The botched delivery."

"Not botched. *Destined*." Ben reached over her lap and grabbed her other hand. Now they were turned toward each other, face to face. Close enough to kiss if the moment ever felt quite right. "You were the answer to my prayer," he said. "You were the hope I needed. And now I don't feel afraid anymore. I bet that sounds pretty ridiculous."

"No, *I love it*," she whispered, wondering whether she were also starting to maybe love him as well. "Thank you for telling me. I wish I weren't afraid anymore."

"Then don't be." Ben popped to his feet and pulled Summer up with him. He cupped his hands around his mouth and shouted into the night, "I'm not afraid anymore!"

Turning back to her, he said, "This feels *awesome*. C'mon. You try it."

"I'm not afraid to live my life!" she yelled toward the stars.

"I'm not afraid to chase my dreams!" he raised his voice louder with each word.

She giggled, having come up with an idea she rather liked, and shouted, "I'm not afraid to take a leap of faith!"

But then there was Ben, pulling her closer, saying, "I'm not afraid to show you how I feel."

They both fell quiet, breathing in sync with one another, their hearts racing from the excitement of it all. And then he bent forward and brushed his lips against hers. Their first kiss, a beautiful kiss. It all felt so... empowering, which is not a word Summer would have thought she'd ever use to describe a romantic moment like this one.

"I can do anything!" She climbed onto the bridge railing and stood teetering above Ben. "I'm not afraid to take a leap of faith!"

She pushed off from the railing and dove into the lake below, letting the air carry her, feeling so alive, so unfettered. A moment later, Ben jumped too.

They were no longer afraid, for they'd found strength in each other.

Chapter 19

The next morning, a beam of light fell into Ben's eyes and woke him up. He brought his fingers to his lips, remembering the beautiful dream he'd just had, the dream in which he'd kissed Summer and she'd kissed him right back. He wanted to lie there forever, basking in that place where dreams still felt like reality, never fully waking up to face the actual truth of his life.

Snap, fizz, crunch.

The symphony of his mother's drinking and doing God knew what else brought him into the real world far too soon for his liking.

"Just another day," he grumbled to himself as he rolled out of bed. His bare toes squished into the cold, wet clothing he'd shrugged out of the night before.

The night before, the actual night, not a dream. He'd kissed Summer, and together they'd jumped from the bridge into the lake below—a leap of faith. No, it wasn't a dream. It only *felt* too good to be true.

Finally. For the first time since Stephen had died, Ben felt like he had something worth living for—something to be truly thankful for—and her name was Summer.

"You really did hear my prayer," he said aloud to whomever was there listening, waiting in the wings to help steer his life back on course. To Jesus, maybe. "Thank you," he whispered, knowing then that the simple words would never be enough. His prayer, his wish, *his life.* He needed to say thank you in a way that meant something. He needed to go to God, just as God had come to him. Which meant church.

Luckily, today was a Sunday.

He quickly dressed in his second nicest outfit, seeing as his nicest was still lying soggy across the floor. A quick spritz of cologne and a little gel in his hair would have to be enough. He'd need the rest of his time to make his mother presentable and drag her out of the house. Hopefully she was sober enough to make the short walk. It only seemed natural that part of taking his life back would have to include helping his mother take control of hers.

As he'd feared, he found her sitting at the kitchen table, still clearly inebriated from the night before. She had a large mixing bowl in front of her and mumbled to herself as she poured a can of beer over cornflakes, mixing them both together in that gigantic bowl.

"Not today," he said, striding over and grabbing away the bowl before Susan could drink her breakfast.

"*Hey*, give that back!" she argued, losing steam with each word.

Ben dumped the entire thing into the sink. "Sorry, Mom, but you need to get dressed."

"I don't *need* to do anything," she grumbled. "*I'm* the parent here. You have to listen to me, not the other way around."

He could see this situation would require a little finessing, so finesse he would. He sat down across from her at the table and waited for her to fix her eyes on him. "Yes" he said. "And I did listen to you and you were right about everything."

"Good. I knew it." She nodded and smiled despite an emptiness that remained in her eyes. Sure enough, she asked a moment later, "Err, about what?"

"Summer," he answered, remembering once again the perfect night they'd shared, wanting so many more evenings like that, but knowing he first had to pay a visit to the man who'd made it all possible. "We had the most awesome date last night, all because of you. Thank you, Mom. Really."

"Oh, you're welcome. Can I have my bowl back, please?" She'd clearly already forgotten that he'd tossed the whole thing down the drain.

"You helped me. Now I'm going to help you. Besides I have more than just you to thank."

"That's okay. I'm good here."

He said another quick prayer, silently. God could read his thoughts, right? *Please, please help her to get through this service without embarrassing herself. Give her the strength to make it just a couple hours. She needs this. She needs you.*

"C'mon, Mom," he said, tugging at her arm. "We're going to church."

From the moment Summer stepped foot in the First Street Church, she was surrounded by an enthusiastic group of local women, most of whom she'd gotten to know well on karaoke night.

"I'm so glad you made it!" Elise crooned, rushing over and running her hands through Summer's freshly teased curls.

"And you look so pretty." Jennifer pulled Summer away from Elise and wrapped her in a tight hug.

"I think what the girls are trying to say," Maisie said, with a roll of her eyes, "is welcome to our church. We're so glad to have you!"

"Nice to see you again, Summer." Kristina Rose grabbed both of Summer's hands and gave them a tight squeeze.

Summer was glad she'd decided to come that morning. It would have been so easy to sleep late and bask in the memories of her date with Ben the night before, but something he'd said had stuck with her. He'd said they were destined to meet, that Summer was the literal answer to his prayer. Summer hadn't said any prayers herself, but did that matter? If God was truly all-powerful, then he had to have known what she needed before she even came close to figuring it out. What if Ben, too, was the answer to her unspoken prayers? And, if so, what did that mean for her future?

This particular revelation provided more questions than it did answers—and that was exactly why she had come to the little white church on First Street. To find those answers.

"Looks like you're not the only new arrival," Kristina said, motioning with her chin toward the front door.

Summer followed her line of sight, but before her eyes even locked on the man and woman who stood there, she knew who to expect.

Ben stood proudly beside his mother, her arm looped in his. Both Davises were scrubbed and polished, blinking as their eyes adjusted to the fluorescent interior lights of the grand foyer. Their eyes connected across the crowded space, and Summer felt as if they were Romeo and Juliet finding each other for the first time at that fancy Capulet party.

Ben smiled at her, the biggest smile she'd seen from him yet—one that showed all his straight, gleaming teeth. He nodded and waved, as if to say, "Look how in sync we are. Somehow I knew I'd find you here."

"Oh, looks like we're getting ready to begin. C'mon!" Elise grabbed Summer's hand and pulled her into the sanctuary. And even though she'd have liked to sit with Ben and Susan, Summer felt as if she were in exactly the right place as the music of the band swelled around her, and the people of Sweet Grove began to lift their voices to Heaven.

So this is what it felt like to belong…

Chapter 20

Much to Ben's delight, his mother managed to sit still through the entire Sunday service. The pastor had chosen that day to teach about the parable of the loaves and fish, one Ben remembered vaguely from an illustrated Bible his mother had given him many Christmases ago.

"The story of the loaves and fish serves as a reminder," the pastor summarized. "Make the most of what you have today, and you will be blessed immeasurably. Let us pray."

After the pastor had given his final blessing, Ben went to seek out Summer. He found her standing near the sound booth, flanked on either side by the women who'd been his classmates growing up.

Maisie saw him first. "Oh, hi, Ben!" she said with an enthusiastic wave.

"Ben?" Elise greeted him with a reserved smile. "It's good to see you here."

"We were just talking about Pastor Bernie's sermon. What did you think?" Kristina Rose asked.

Ben pushed into the group beside Summer and laced his fingers through hers, a gesture that did not go unnoticed.

"Aww!" Jennifer squealed. "You two are so cute!"

Summer leaned her head against Ben's shoulder as if to claim him. He liked that very much. Her friends, it seemed, did too.

"Too cute! Too cute!" Elise and Jennifer chanted, then burst apart in giggles.

"Now that I see you two together," Maisie added. "I don't know why I didn't realize sooner that you'd be so good for each other. I'm really happy for you, Ben."

"I'm really happy for me, too." He squeezed Summer's hand, and she squeezed his back. "And to answer your earlier question, it was an awesome sermon. Just what I needed today."

"I've taught about this parable before with my youth group," Elise said, and then dove into a more pedantic examination of the sermon.

Ben decided to take that opportunity to ask Summer a question. "Would you care to accompany me and my mother to Sunday Brunch?"

"Depends. Are you asking me out on a *date* date?" She whispered the question into his ear so as not to be rude to the others.

He turned and put his mouth against the soft flesh of her lobe. "*Yes*. And this time without prompting from either of the women in my life."

"Well, in that case…" Summer let go of his hand and wrapped Jennifer in a hug. Jennifer, Ben noted, was perhaps the huggiest person he'd ever come across.

"Are you heading home?" the Sunday school teacher asked.

"Something like that. We'll see you all soon, okay?"

"Oooh, you're a 'we' now. I love it!" Jennifer squealed, then gave Ben a hug too.

"Hope to see you next week—same time, same place," Maisie called as Ben and Summer walked away, holding firmly onto each other's hands.

They found Ben's mother talking with Sheriff Grant just outside the front door and dragged her along to Summer's sedan rather than asking her to walk the short distance to Mabel's on Maple. Ben and

Summer chatted the whole way over, but Susan kept mostly to herself.

After placing their order for pancakes and orange juice all around, Ben decided to pull his mother into the conversation, rather than letting her shrink back into herself. "Did you like the sermon, Mom?"

Susan ran her finger around the rim of her glass and shrugged. "It was fine, I guess. But it's hard to make the most of what you've got when you've got a whole lot of nothing."

Ben frowned.

Nothing, huh? Is that what I am to my own mother? Is this why I've hated my life? I wasn't valued, so I didn't assign myself value? Which psychologist said that? Jung? Maslow? Freud?

Ben glanced at Summer, the shining beacon of hope in his otherwise dark life. The hope that had literally pulled him back from death.

"What did you think of the music?" she asked his mother.

"Oh, yes, the singing was nice." Susan smiled and politely answered Summer's various questions until the food came and she closed up again.

Summer is my future, he told himself. Does that mean my mother is my past? He eyed each woman in turn, a realization striking him in that moment.

It was exactly as Summer had said the evening before. He did have an angel and a devil on either shoulder. One represented encouragement, love, happiness, joy and endless possibilities, *loaves and fishes.* The other was only self-destruction. His angel and devil weren't cartoons though, they were real—and, for better or worse, they were his.

But he didn't have to be a bystander. He could take an active role in his own life. It was time he did just that. He could help his mother, so blinded by past grief she couldn't see the blessings before her now. And he could help Summer, so afraid of the future that she had trouble seeing her own amazingness.

With God giving him strength, he didn't need to wait for a hero. Instead, he could be one himself.

The homemade apple butter at Mabel's on Maple was simply to die for, but then again that's what you got when the main pride and joy of a town was its historic apple grove. Summer had to force herself to slow down long enough between bites to carry the conversation forward.

Ben seemed to have gotten lost in his thoughts partway through their meal, and it was never easy carrying on a coherent discussion with Susan, but a challenge was okay. Summer liked having to work to bring people out of their shells. She'd always been great with people. That was the one thing she knew for sure about herself—she was a people person.

Ben, on the other hand, tended to grow even more reserved whenever she had to share his company with Susan. He was an introvert to begin with, and adding the anchor of his family's shared grief pulled him even deeper into himself.

She liked the new side of Ben she'd seen these past couple days, maybe even loved it. Would he be his best self always from now on, or at least more often? She hoped she could help both him and Susan find the peace they so desperately needed, and she also hoped that things would work out for all of them in the end, even though with her uncertain future and their unattractive past, she had no idea how that would happen.

Faith. That's what she needed, and that's why she'd ventured to church that morning.

"I've got to run to the little girls' room now," Susan announced loudly as she rose to her feet and trotted away from their table.

This was her chance to draw Ben back out of the darkness he'd began to disappear into. She rummaged in her purse until she found a stray coin. A dime.

"Penny for your thoughts," she said, sliding it in front of Ben with one firm finger.

"You do realize that's a dime, right?" A smile played at the corners of Ben's mouth, and just like that, he returned to her.

She winked at him and said, "So you can owe me more thoughts later. Get talking, bub."

He let out a slow breath and Summer's anxiety spiked.

"Oh, please tell me it's not that bad!"

He chuckled. "It's not bad at all. I was just thinking how glad I am that you came to help your Aunt Iris this summer. And…"

"And?" *Wait, that's not bad at all. Why did I assume he'd gone to a dark place?*

"*And…*" Ben leaned over to her and whispered the last part directly into her ear, "I'll have to owe you on those other nine thoughts. I'm working on an idea, and I'll need your help when it's ready."

"That sounds ominous."

"Maybe it is. Maybe it isn't. I guess you'll just have to wait and see." He cleared his throat and took a long drink of juice.

Susan returned from the restroom and plopped into her chair, immediately picking up her fork and digging back into the syrup-soaked stack of pancakes before her. "So what did I miss?" she asked.

And what did I miss? Summer wondered. She couldn't wait to learn more about Ben's plan—or God's, for that matter.

Good things are coming. Faith.

Chapter 21

On Monday morning, Ben got dressed quickly. He'd taken too many days off from work lately, and although Maisie said she didn't mind—was, in fact, happy he was taking some time for himself—he still feared letting her down. Especially since he had such a big favor to ask of her that day.

He peeked into his mother's room, but she hadn't made it to bed the evening before. He found her curled up on the couch under an old afghan with empty beer bottles strewn across the carpet at her side.

"I'm going to work now, Mom," he said, touching his lips to her forehead.

When she didn't stir, he added, "I'll be home soon. Have a good day. Love you."

Still no response from his mother, but he hoped she had heard. She needed to know that he loved her, and he needed to make sure he told her more often. Love had saved his life. Now maybe it could save hers, too.

With one last glance toward the sleeping form of his mother, he headed through the door and out into the day. It was a big day, and quite possibly a great one.

Only Maisie could decide that now.

He murmured a prayer as he made his way down Cypress street. "God?" he asked tentatively. Although he had since become sure that there was a God up there who looked out for him, he still wasn't exactly sure the best way to talk to him. These things would take practice, he supposed.

And Ben was good at practice, thanks to his long sports career in school. "God," he started again. "When I was ready to give up, you helped me. You picked me up and gave me a reason to keep going. And I think that maybe you helped simply because I was brave enough to ask. But my mom..." He paused here and sighed. "She doesn't ask for help. The only thing she asks for is alcohol." He choked out a laugh in order to keep from crying. The bitter truth of these words hurt, but they needed to be said.

"I haven't been the best at this whole prayer thing," he continued. "Or religion or church or any of it. But you helped me anyway. Now, if it's all right, I'd like to ask for just one more favor. Use me to help my mom. Give me the right words. Give me the strength. I helped her sink so low into herself, and now I need your help to lift her up again. *Help me to help her.* I believe you can do it. Thank you."

Ben ended his prayer just moments before arriving at the market. As he expected, Maisie was already there, merrily arranging a display of brightly colored fruits and vegetables.

"Good morning!" she trilled as he strode through the sliding glass doors. "I'm glad you're here early, because I want to hear all about you and Summer. Seriously, Ben, I'm so happy for you both."

Just the mention of Summer's name put a smile on his face.

Maisie saw that too. "Oh, you are absolutely smitten. I love it, Ben! You deserve this!"

He brought a hand to the back of his neck and looked away. He could talk about Summer all day and still not have fully expressed all the things she had come to mean to him, but today couldn't be about Summer. It had to be about helping his mom.

Maisie's face fell. She came over and laid a hand on his shoulder, speaking softly to him. "Oh, Ben. What's wrong?"

"Nothing's wrong. At least nothing new. I… Maisie, I have a really big favor to ask. Before you answer though, will you please hear me out?"

"Of course I will. C'mon, let's go sit in my office." She waited for Ben to file in after her, then grabbed a stack of mismatched flyers from the chair and plopped them on her already messy desk. "Sorry, sorry," she chattered. "With Iris out of town, the notices for our cork board have just been stacking up. If she doesn't make it back too, I'm going to need to invest in a second one. Who knew gossip was the oil that kept this whole town running smoothly? Okay, there. Sit."

Ben nervously accepted the chair, then cleared his throat and jumped into explaining the idea he'd been formulating in his mind since the previous afternoon at brunch—the same idea he'd hinted at to Summer.

"Maisie, you've been really good to me over the years," he said. "You've given me a job. You've been a friend, even when I wasn't much of one in return, and I know it's not fair to ask you for anything more than you've already given me, but…" He took a deep breath in through his nose. "But my mom needs help. She's needed help for a long time, and I finally feel brave enough to make sure she gets it. But the thing is…"

"Ben…" Maisie pushed a stack of receipts aside and sat down on top of her desk. It seemed like she had more to say, but now that he'd begun his speech, he wanted to get it all out before he lost the nerve. He looked away and spoke quickly as he ran through the rest of his request.

"The thing is, she needs professional help, and that's expensive. I don't have much of anything saved up, but if you could give me an advance on my next few paychecks, then I would work extra shifts to pay it back as fast as I could. You don't have to give me an answer now, but I was hoping—"

She stood again and placed a hand on each arm of the chair, forcing him to look at her straight on. "Ben, stop. How much do you need?"

"Five thousand," he said, trying—and failing—to avoid her gaze. "Five thousand. *At least.* I know it's a lot, but…" The words were starting to run together, and it sounded more like *I'll-pay-it-back-as-soon-as-I-can.*

Maisie sat back down, began rummaging through her desk drawers in search of something. "Five thousand dollars is more than just a couple extra shifts, Ben. It will take you ages to pay it back."

Oh, no. He'd really thought she would agree to his plan. He had it all laid out logically. It made sense, but without Maisie's support, he'd hit a dead end. "I know it's a lot," he agreed. "But I don't have any other—"

"So don't." She pulled out an old metal safe and set it atop the desk.

"P-pardon?"

"Look at me, Ben. Your mom was my favorite teacher growing up. I love her. This town loves her. But when we lost your brother, God rest his soul, it's like we lost her too. I understand the situation you're in, Ben, but I can't grant your request for a pay advance."

He tried to hide his frown, but it seemed Maisie saw through him anyway. "Oh," he said. "Umm. Okay. I guess I'll—"

"No, stop. Listen to me, Ben. I'm giving you the money, but it's not a loan, it's not an advance. It's a gift."

"Maisie, I couldn't possibly!"

"Hush now, you can and you will." She grabbed a stack of bills from the safe and pressed them into Ben's hands. The large wad of money felt light, insignificant, atop his palms—far too small to be the answer to all his problems. Yet here it was. Here he was. Tears of joy threatened to spill, but he sucked them back in as Maisie continued to speak, a huge smile splashed across her face.

"This town has been trying to heal from that day for far too long. And none of us will ever be able to move past the loss of your brother until your mother does. I'm going to write you a check right now. Take it and go. Take as many days as you need. Go get your mother the help she needs."

Ben quickly wiped at the corners of his eyes with the backs of his hands. The tears had gotten away from him again, those tricky little things. "I'm sorry, I just…"

"*Shh.* We know, Ben. There's not a lick of shame in asking for help. I'm just glad I'm in a position to give back to a woman that gave me so much. I've been praying for you both so long, and finally God has given us the answer we wanted to hear."

"Thank you," Ben choked out—both to Maisie and God. "Thank you so much."

"You're welcome. Now go. Go, make things the way they should be."

Ben rushed out of the store and sprinted over to Morning Glory's, where Summer had only just begun to set up shop for the day. If she was surprised to see him, she didn't show it.

"Why hello, stranger," she said with a mock forties accent as she raced over to press a kiss to his lips. Ben gave himself a moment to delight in her sweet kisses, but only just a single moment.

He pulled away and brushed a tendril of hair from Summer's cheek. "Hey, good looking," he said with a bit of a swagger. "Whaddaya say we blow this popsicle stand, eh?"

Summer laughed and wrapped her arms around him. "You don't mean…?"

"I mean, see! Yeah!" He kissed her again, because he just couldn't help himself.

She ran her fingers through his hair. "So now you're Clyde, and I'm Bonnie." She gave him another affectionate peck. "But, actually, I have no idea what you mean. Did you take the day off?"

He picked her up and set her on the counter. "I did, and I want you to, too."

Now Summer's brow creased in confusion. "But, Ben, I'm only just opening."

He took the wad of bills from his pocket and fanned them in front of her.

"Wow, now wait a minute. I was only joking about being Bonnie and Clyde. You didn't rob a bank, did you?"

He raised an eyebrow. "I think you know me better than that," he said firmly, but then collapsed into a laugh of his own. "Where are my manners? Summer, my lady, would you please escort me to the noble city of Austin on this here beautiful morning?"

"Ben? What have you got planned for us?"

"Not just us, but my mom too. Remember that idea I mentioned? We're going to help her, Summer. Just like you always wanted, but I was too afraid, and I didn't know how. Now I know how, and Maisie is helping too. But Mom doesn't know, so we're going to have to trick her, I think. How good are you at acting?"

"You mean actressing?"

He shrugged. "Sure. How good are you at *actressing?*"

"Actressing was my minor in college, so pretty darned good. What do we need to do?"

"Give me one day. Just today. Close the shop, and help me. I need you with me today."

"Of course, Ben. I'm here. *Always.*"

He paused for a moment to wonder at her words, but they only had a short amount of time if they were going to pull this whole thing off without a hitch.

"I have some people to talk to. I need you on the front lines. Can you go to my house and distract my mom? Keep her busy and make sure she doesn't suspect anything. Sneak in and pack a bag for her if you can. She'll need it, because she's got a long stay.

Three months. But that's all it will take to give her *her* life back. Are you with me?"

"Always," Summer said, then flipped the open sign over and locked the door to the flower shop.

"Always," she repeated as they got into her car and drove.

Chapter 22

Summer had come up with the perfect way to distract Susan and even to get her to pack her own bags to boot.

"Susan! Susan! Are you here? I've got great news!" she shouted as she pushed through the front door then shot around the living room, thrusting blinds open.

Ben's mother sat up on the couch and rubbed the sleep from her eyes. From the looks of it, she'd had a rough night. "Ben? You're home already?"

Summer needed to put on her cheeriest voice if this ruse was going to work. She'd promised Ben her *actressing* skills would get the job done, and now it was time to get to work. "Not Ben. *Summer*," she shouted. "Get up! Get up! We only have a little while to get ready!"

Susan looked unimpressed. "I'm not going anywhere at the butt crack of dawn. Come back later."

But Summer, not to be put off so easily, strode over and yanked the reluctant woman to her feet. "You don't understand. We have to go now. Well, as soon as Ben comes back with the tickets anyway!"

Now she had Susan's attention. "Tickets? What tickets?"

"To the concert, silly! Didn't Ben tell you we won tickets on the radio? We're going to see Carrie Underwood live!"

Susan yawned and scratched at her scalp. "We are?"

Summer nodded vigorously as she picked up the empty bottles and took them to the kitchen. "And it's not just Carrie. There's a whole country music festival, and we get to stay for the entire thing. The radio is even springing for a fancy hotel! Now pack your bags, go. We have to be ready when Ben gets back."

It took a little more than an hour for Ben to return, but Summer managed to keep Susan busy by asking for voice lessons so she could sing along with Carrie and not embarrass herself.

"Are we ready?" Ben asked as he came inside and gave his mother a quick peck on the cheek.

"I can't believe I get to see all my favorite singers live," Susan said. She'd taken a dose of extra strength

Tylenol and was looking much more alive than she had when Summer had first burst through the doors.

"What?" Ben asked innocently.

"The concert, Ben. *Remember?*" Summer said between gritted teeth. It looked like Ben's acting skills needed a bit more work.

"Oh, oh, right. The concert. Well, we better get going so we don't miss the opening act. Are you ready, ladies?"

He pushed his palm into his forehead with a bit more dramatic flair than seemed natural. Thankfully his mother was far too excited to notice.

A moment later, the three of them piled into Summer's car and hit the road for Austin. Summer hooked her iPhone up to an auxiliary cable and put on her country music playlist, and together she and Susan belted out each song as its twangy beats filled the sedan. Even Ben joined in for a special rendition of "Live like you were Dying" by Tim McGraw. Summer was pleasantly surprised to find he'd inherited some of his mother's musical talent.

After what felt like no time at all, they pulled up to a large medical facility and parked the car. The mood immediately changed.

"What's this? This isn't the concert," Susan grumbled.

"Just a pit stop, Mom." Ben got out of the car and grabbed Susan's luggage from the trunk.

She shook her head adamantly. "If it's a pit stop then why are you taking my bags? And why does that sign say Austin Rehabilitation Center?"

Summer braced herself for the argument she'd known was coming. "I'm sorry, Susan. We didn't mean to trick you, but—"

"Yes, you did! *You did mean to!* You planned this behind my back, lied to my face. I'm not going in there!" She made wide sweeping gestures with her hands as she spoke, then crossed her arms over her chest like a petulant child.

Ben slammed the trunk shut. His face looked more angry than sympathetic. "Don't talk to her like that, Mom. It's not her fault. I was the one—"

Summer raised her hand to silence Ben before he could say anything more, then turned in her seat to face his mother. "You're right, Susan. We *did* trick you, but only because we didn't know how else we could help. These past few weeks I have loved getting to know both you and Ben and, heck, the whole town of Sweet Grove too. But did you know that, at times, it's like you're two different people? There's the woman I saw this morning who patiently taught me to sing my favorite song even though we both know I can't carry a tune to save my life."

She paused a moment, fixing a big smile on Susan, but the other woman couldn't even be bothered to look at Summer. She did, however, seem to be paying rapt attention, so Summer took a deep breath and continued. "Then there's the woman who was so drunk out of her mind that first night we met that she tried to pick a fight with me and my friends in the middle of a bar."

She saw Ben's form move in her peripheral vision, but all of Summer's attention was focused on Susan, on watching for the exact moment her words hit home. Oh, how she prayed they would hit the needed mark.

"There's the woman who makes jokes and pays compliments, but there's also the one who is angry, who tries to hide behind a bottle of booze every waking moment of the day. And, remember, *you* tricked Ben to get us together. You tricked him, and it worked. You tricked him, not to be mean, but because you love him, and you could see what was best for him even if he couldn't yet see it for himself. And, Susan, he loves you right on back and he wants more of you— the real you. Not the woman who picks fights in bars or needs a drink to get up and face the morning. He's been there for you all these years. Now he's asking you—*I'm asking you*—can you be there for him?"

Susan uncrossed her arms and wrung her hands in her lap. She chewed on her lower lip. Maybe because she craved a drink and needed to keep her mouth busy. Maybe to keep from speaking too soon and saying something she would regret.

When it became clear that she was not going to speak just yet, Ben leaned in through the open car window and handed his mother a stack of cards. "I asked Summer to keep you busy this morning so I could work on getting these," he explained. "Go on, open them."

Susan's hand shook as she opened the first envelope, a cheery pink one with her name written in large, loopy letters. She pulled out a Hallmark card with a cartoon apple on the front. It had a hot water bottle and a thermometer sticking from its illustrated mouth. *Get Well Soon*, the front read.

Inside there was a handwritten note and a signature that appeared to say Maisie Bryant. Summer tried not to stare. Susan needed this moment for herself, but as Susan read, Summer picked up bits and pieces of what each card said.

We lost more than Stephen that day, Maisie's message

read. *You've already lost one son. Don't lose the other by forgetting about him.*

Susan sniffed and tucked the card back into its envelope and then opened up the next one. This one had a pair of orange kittens on its front and a message from Jennifer inside. *You are my hero. You're the reason I became a teacher too. I am praying that you will find your fire again.*

She dabbed at the corners of her eyes and opened the next card from Pastor Bernie. *God never gives us more than we can handle, but sometimes we all need help to see His plan. Sweet Grove loves you and wants you back. May His grace shine upon you.*

Susan's tears fell freely by the time she reached a card from Sheriff Grant. *I miss seeing you smile, Susan. Do whatever it takes to get that smile back.*

She continued to flip through the cards, opening each one and taking time to digest the message inside. When she had finished, Ben handed her one last card. This one rested in a plain white envelope. The card inside had no frills or intricate designs. Its surface was glossy, bright yellow.

Susan opened it and a picture fell out into her lap. It showed a young boy Summer instantly recognized as Ben. Standing beside him was a slightly older boy with darker hair and eyes, but the same smile. A more youthful version of Susan squatted down beside them, a huge, joyful smile on her pretty face. She fingered each of the three figures in turn as if caressing them could bring back that innocent time, the time before their lives had all changed irreparably.

"Do it for Stephen," Ben said. "He'd want you to get better. I want you to get better. Please, Mom. Can't we be a family again?"

Chapter 23

Ben's first night at home without his mother had been the most difficult.

"You miss her," Summer said, pulling him in for a cuddle and stroking his hair as she spoke to him.

Ben sighed. Why was it that only one part of his life could be right at any given time? Then again, before Summer, his world had been in complete disarray. At least he was making progress now, striding toward a better life one step at a time.

"I didn't realize it would be this hard," he admitted. "What am I going to do without her for three whole months?"

Summer smiled and mussed up his hair. "Well, you've got me for almost two of them. I'll make sure you don't get lonely."

He kissed her then, ending that particular conversation. Both knew where it could lead, and neither wanted to go there.

The issue, however, remained. What *would* happen once Iris returned and Summer was no longer needed to run the flower shop? Ben couldn't think about that just then, or the sadness and uncertainly of his life would drag him into the darkness once again.

Now that he'd seen the light of Summer, he only wanted to bask in her warmth. It all had to work out in the end, didn't it? God wouldn't have answered Ben's prayer only to change His mind and take it all away again. Even though Ben was new to this whole faith thing, he simply couldn't believe in a God who would play such cruel games. And so he remained hopefully—perhaps even *foolishly*—optimistic, brushing the thought of ever losing Summer so far to the side that, with time, it didn't even register anymore.

That is, until the truth came crashing back and knocked Ben clean off his feet.

Several weeks had passed, and he and Summer had

spent every single one of them wrapped in each other's arms or walking hand in hand through the town of Sweet Grove. Even though he missed his mother, he loved the new shape his life had taken. He loved Summer, and he told her every chance he had.

Everything had changed, though, on one ordinary August day. He'd finished his shift at the market, and rather than head to the library as was once his routine, he now came to Morning Glory's to help Summer finish her work for the day and close up shop.

When he arrived, he found Summer talking on the phone with her back turned away from the door. He came up to hug her hips from behind, but she brushed him away.

"Yes, yes, thank you. Yes, I'll see you then. Thank you so much for this opportunity," she said, then hung up her phone. This call hadn't been with a customer ordering flowers. Ben's heart churned in his chest. *Oh, no. Oh, no. Not yet. Please God, not ever.*

She turned to face him, a deep frown marring her beautiful face.

"We both knew this couldn't last forever," she started, and Ben knew that his worst fears—his fears that were so terrible he couldn't even fully acknowledge them—had officially come to light. "As much as we may have wanted it to. There's no place for me here, Ben."

The sudden declaration shocked him so much, he needed to take a seat, to brace himself for this conversation—the conversation he had foolishly believed wasn't coming. "Yes, there is a place," he insisted. "Right here with me, the man who loves you."

"Ben, don't." She lifted her hand and clutched at her forehead as if fending off the world's worst migraine.

He wanted to go to her, to hold her, to tell her to stay, but he was so afraid of what happened next and he couldn't stand the thought of her pushing him away. Instead he chose to focus on the facts. "Don't you love me too?"

She shook her head then sighed, still unwilling to look into his eyes. "You know I do," she said. "And if you really do love me don't make this harder than it needs to be. Can you do that for me?"

"I don't understand. Everything was great yesterday. Who was that on the phone? What changed today? And how can we *un*change it?"

She dropped her hand from her face, and Ben saw her eyes were rimmed with red—though not a tear fell. "My Aunt Iris is coming home tonight."

Could it really be? Had so much time passed

already? Somehow it felt like Summer had been with him forever, but at the same time as if they'd only just gotten started. This couldn't be it. This couldn't be the end. He wanted to tell her all these things, but instead he simply said, "Oh, I see."

Summer paced the length of the shop, filling the small storefront with a cloud of nervous energy. "She'll take over the shop again, and there will be nothing left for me to do. We both know I'd only get in her way," she explained. "And I can't just sit around the house all day, Ben. I need to be out among people. I need to have a purpose."

He nodded. He knew all this about her, but he still didn't know why she couldn't stay right here with him. She was the answer to his prayer. Forever and ever, amen. God had sent her to save him and his mother. What would happen to them without her?

"Where will you go?" he asked, still unable to say the most important things that ran through his mind.

"I just accepted a job in Portland, doing administrative work at a law firm. I leave the day after tomorrow." She picked up a small paper weight from the table and tossed it from hand to hand, then resumed pacing.

"Administrative work? Law firm? That's not right for you at all."

"But what choice have I got, Ben? I have to do something with my life."

He stood and hoped she would stop pacing long enough for him to gather her in his arms, but she just kept walking back and forth, just kept walking away from him, from the future he so desperately wanted them to have together. *"Stay here*, Summer," he pleaded. "The people of this town love you. *I* love you."

She stopped pacing but did not come into his arms. Instead she hung her head and spoke woodenly. "You know I can't stay. If I stayed and did nothing, refused to face my fears, I wouldn't be the woman you fell in love with anymore, now would I?"

"Then let me come with you!"

"You know you can't do that, Ben. Your mom will be back in just over a month. She needs you now more than ever."Summer was right about that—no matter how wrong she was now about everything else.

"But what about what *I* need?" he argued.

"I'm sorry," she mumbled. "I wouldn't be true to myself if I stayed, and I wouldn't be good enough for you either."

"But—"

She raised her hand to stop him from saying anything more.

"Ben, I can't. Not right now. Not anymore. Can we

just—? Can you help me close up here? We can talk about this more later. It still hasn't all quite sunken in."

He agreed to drop the topic and dutifully helped her shut down the flower shop for the night. But everything she'd just said wounded him deeply.

How could she possibly think she wasn't good enough for him? Or that she had to leave in order to make herself better? She was already the best thing to ever happen in his life. After all, *he* was the one with no education and a dead-end job. She was already too good for him, but rather than question how they'd ended up together, he'd instead chosen to appreciate it, to be thankful. What if once Summer had done all she needed to do to make herself "good enough for him", she no longer felt he was good enough for her?

His head spun with all the implications.

He didn't care if he had to give up on his dream of going to school and becoming a history teacher altogether. Now a life with Summer was the only dream that mattered, and it was quickly slipping from his grasp.

How could he convince her to stay? He had to come up with something. And fast.

The rest of his life depended on it.

If being in love was the best thing Summer had ever felt, breaking Ben's heart was by far the worst—especially since she'd had to break her own, too. But they had brought this on themselves, hadn't they?

Yes.

She'd spent every free moment in his arms these past couple months. Partially because she worried about him being alone while his mother served out her stint in rehab, but mostly because being in his arms felt like exactly where she needed to be.

Unfortunately, *Ben's girlfriend* wasn't exactly an occupation she could put on business cards. She needed a job—a career—and she'd neglected that fact for far too long. In hindsight, she should have been continuing her job search—and her soul search—that entire summer in Sweet Grove, checking out books like *What Color is Your Parachute?*, browsing the listings online, working her network to see what she could find, even exploring possible graduate programs that might have a place for her.

But she hadn't done any of that. Mostly because it had been far too easy to push aside these unpleasant tasks and instead kick back and enjoy her new relationship with Ben.

Faith, she'd told herself. But she realized now that faith wasn't just about sitting back and waiting for good to come to you. It was also about being willing to take that leap, about being willing to charge after what you wanted. She'd understood that too late to change things now, and she needed to make up for lost time however she could.

That's why when a recruiter called her with a job opening in Portland, she'd taken their series of quick telephone interviews. And when a few short days later, the company called to make a formal offer, she'd accepted it sight unseen and without a moment's hesitation. After all, no one else was making her any offers—and she couldn't live on love alone, as much as she wished she could find a way to do just that.

She hadn't hesitated, but by now she'd second-guessed herself plenty. But no matter how she turned the problem over in her mind, she always came up with the same solution. She needed to leave.

Yet again, she ran through an endless series of what-if scenarios as she drove to pick Aunt Iris up from the airport. She thought back to her first meeting with Ben, their afternoon at the wishing well, their pledge to stop being afraid taken atop the cider mill bridge—she thought about every moment in between, and every moment since.

Still, if she could do it all over again, she wouldn't change a single thing.

The love that had bloomed between them was a gift she'd forever cherish, even when she and Ben had long since moved on to their real lives. Maybe he could start things up again with Elise—or even Sally. For as crazy as the librarian came across, she clearly had strong feelings for Ben. And why wouldn't she?

Ben was *awesome*.

So awesome, in fact, that she knew he would find a way to be okay without her. He had to, because she was leaving town. Did he understand that she didn't have a choice in the matter either? Would he forgive her for allowing herself to fall so head over heels in love and for dragging him down with her?

Oh, if only Portland weren't so far from Sweet Grove. But it *was* far, too far. Then again, if they were meant to be together, it would eventually work out, right? Maybe once she had a bit of experience under her belt, she could find a job somewhere closer. Maybe Austin. And maybe if Ben wasn't…

Oh, who was she kidding? Certainly not herself, and not Ben either.

Why had she been so foolish? Why had she allowed herself to fall in love, to envision a future with Ben, when she'd always known it couldn't end any other way than this?

She would hate herself a little bit forever for having done this to him, but life was about the journey, not the destination, and her train was getting ready to pull out of the station.

She pulled up to the arrival gate and watched as stranger after stranger poured from the airport. She smiled sadly to herself as the returning travelers leaped into the arms of the loved ones who'd missed them. Would she ever find a love like that again? Or had she already used up her one chance for greatness?

Aunt Iris emerged from the double sliding doors, weighted down by two huge suitcases and a duffel bag. The moment she spied Summer, a huge smile crept across her tanned face, and for the briefest of seconds, Summer forgot her troubles and just felt happy.

She jumped out of the car, leaving it to idle at the curb, and ran to hug her aunt. She hadn't realized until now how much she had missed Iris.

"It's so good to see you, Sunny Summer," Iris cooed. "I have so much to tell you and Sunny Sunshine about my trip. So many pictures to share."

But then the reality of her situation struck again, and Summer couldn't keep it in anymore. She hugged her aunt as tight as her arms would allow and began to cry huge crocodile tears.

Aunt Iris wasted no time in fishing a hankie from her duffel and dabbing at Summer's wet eyes. "Hey, hey. What's wrong, my beautiful girl?"

"Everything. *Everything* is wrong. I've messed up so bad, Aunt Iris. So bad." She accepted the handkerchief and blew her nose.

"C'mon, c'mon. Let's get you home, and on the way you can tell me everything."

Summer burst into tears anew. *Home.* How she wished Sweet Grove could be that to her, but no. Everything in the tiny town fit just so, and now that the rightful owner of Morning Glory's had returned, there was no place for Summer—or at least no job.

How could she explain to her aunt everything that had happened these past few months? Now that Iris was here at last, Summer just wanted to go home—to her home, *Iris's* home, not Summer's. Not Summer's. *Not Summer's.*

"You know I love you very much, right?" Iris said as she sank behind the driver's seat and transitioned the car into drive.

"Sometimes love isn't enough," Summer croaked, but Aunt Iris wouldn't have any of that.

"Oh, honey. Love is *always* enough."

Chapter 24

Brave. Ben needed to be brave. Not just about trivial things like his choices in reading or trying an exotic new food, but he needed to find the courage to take his life by the reins and steer it to the place he needed to be.

No more wallowing in misery. No more giving up. A lot had changed in the past few months, and it had all been because of the answer God had given to his once desperate prayer. It had all been because of Summer.

Feeling desperate once more, he now dropped on his knees to talk to the God who was no longer a stranger. "If it is Your will, God," he prayed, "guide me. There isn't much time."

He knew that he'd need to be patient. God wasn't a magic eight ball in the sky, after all. His will would be revealed in time. And though Ben put his faith first and foremost in Heaven, there was also a person on Earth who had expertly guided him in his relationship with Summer—and she was only a quick phone call away.

He waited for a few moments after placing the call while the nurse went to fetch his mother.

"Hello?" she answered at last. A wave of relief washed over him, just from hearing her voice.

"*Mom*, how are you doing?" And calling her Mom felt good, right at last.

She chuckled softly. "It gets easier every day."

How would he broach this topic with her? He didn't want to upset her, nor did he want it to seem as if he wasn't also concerned with her recovery. He needed to be delicate. "So it stops hurting after a while, giving up the thing you love?" he said.

"Oh, Ben." His mother sighed. "I didn't love the booze, and the booze definitely didn't love me."

"What do you mean?" He waited for her to explain herself.

"I mean that I used it to hide from the things I really, actually do love—like you, like Stephen's memory."

Here it was, the opening he'd been waiting for—
and so he asked, "How can you *love* a memory?"

"I'm pretty sure you already know exactly what I
mean. Just because someone goes away, that doesn't
mean the love you felt for him goes away too. Feelings
never die, Ben. Even if people sometimes do."

"Mom, I didn't mean to—"

"I know, son. I know. But you don't have to handle
me with kid gloves any longer. I'm getting the help I
need here, thanks to you. I'm learning to live with the
pain rather than hiding from it. But this call isn't about
me, is it? It's about Summer."

"How did you…?"

"She called a few days back. Told me about a job
she'd interviewed for in Portland. Asked me not to say
anything until she had the chance to talk to you
herself. I take it she got it, huh?"

Ben broke down, feeling sorrow but also relief—
relief that he could finally turn to his mother for
strength, that she could now lift him up instead of
always weighing him down. "Mom, what am I going to
do?" he said, choking back a sob.

Susan didn't seem as upset as he'd expected her to
be, though her words remained kind, steady. "You're
going to stop her, obviously."

"Stop her? But how?"

She let out a slow breath. When she spoke again, he could hear a smile behind her words. "I don't know that, but I have a feeling you do."

He shook his head, studied the linoleum on the kitchen floor. "I actually have no idea how I'm going to ask her to give everything up and stay with me."

"*Yes. You. Do.* I'm going to teach you a trick the staff here has taught me. Ben, I need you to close your eyes."

He complied immediately. He didn't have any time to waste wondering what his mother was up to. He needed a solution, and he needed it now. "Okay." Ben took a deep breath.

"Now picture your life five years from now," his mother said. "If you keep going exactly as you are today, what will that life look like?"

Well, this thought exercise was easy. It's something he'd thought of constantly since Summer had said she needed to go. "I'll be alone, working at the grocery store, doing nothing with my life."

"Okay, so that's your reality if you *don't* make a change today. Mine was that I'd still be drunk or possibly dead. Neither sounds so great—your future or mine. We both need a change."

"I agree, but…" He wanted to argue, but he didn't know what else to say. It was time for him to stop talking and just listen.

"Close your eyes again. Now think about your *best* possible life. Try to picture yourself five years from now, having achieved your dreams and being exactly the person you want to be."

"Okay, I'm picturing it."

"Are you alone, working at the grocery store, doing nothing with your life?"

He smiled, trying his best to hold onto the beautiful mental image he'd conjured. "No, I'm with Summer, and I'm happy."

"What else?" his mother prompted.

"I don't work at the grocery store anymore. I'm finally a teacher, like you."

"Are you happy?"

"Yes, very." He opened his eyes again and looked around the barren kitchen, the old house that had been the prison of his unhappiness for so many years past and would be for so many years to come. Just like that, he felt hopeless once more. He watched as his vision of Summer sank deeper and deeper beneath the surface. He groaned and said, "But I can't—"

"Eh, eh, eh!" His mother corrected him. "Saying *but*, saying *I can't* is why you haven't made a change.

It's why you're stuck, Ben. It's why I was stuck. I can't get through the day without a drink. I'll give up booze, but I'll do it tomorrow. I can't. I can't. But, but, but. *You can. You will.* Period."

"It's great you have so much faith in me, Mom, but I still don't know what to do."

"Yes, you do. Picture those two different lives again. What do you have to do to turn the first vision into the second? Can you just snap your fingers and make it so?"

"No, but—"

"*Ben,*" she warned. "No buts. You have to be confident, be brave to make a change. Don't second guess yourself. Don't second guess God's plan. Think about it. Think about how you can turn that first future into the second, better one. You don't need a Band-Aid, Ben. You need a cure. I can't just say I'm going to stop drinking, and—*poof*—I'm cured. I need to do the work. I need to get at the source of *why* I drink and tackle that problem. That's what I have to do to uncover my second future. Do you understand now?"

"I have to fix the reason why I'm losing Summer if I want to keep her?"

"Bingo. So go do it. You haven't got any time to lose. And, Ben?"

"Yeah, Mom?"

"I love you, and you *can* do this." And with that simple affirmation, Ben knew he could make that second future a reality. He could make it *his* future. He just needed to be brave. Needed to stop finding problems and start making solutions.

He could, and he would.

Summer was leaving early the next morning, flying out of Texas and into Oregon—not sure when she'd ever manage to return. Because this was her last full day in Sweet Grove, she planned to spend the entire thing with Ben at her side. After all, she'd be leaving the biggest piece of herself behind in his care—her heart.

She'd spent the following evening catching up with Aunt Iris. It still felt odd, even today. She'd spent so much time living inside her favorite relative's life, but hadn't been able to actually spend any time with her in the flesh until now. Summer only wished she had more time with Iris, with Ben, and with trying to figure things out.

She'd shouted into the night sky all those weeks

ago, saying she wasn't afraid—but that had been a lie, or at least that's the way it seemed now. She was terrified, actually, but she needed to keep moving forward. The future was now. Or at least as soon as she could pull herself out of bed.

A soft knock sounded on her door. Aunt Iris called from the other side, "Good morning, dear. Are you up?"

"Yeah, come in!" Summer sounded as if she had a frog stuck in her throat.

Aunt Iris padded in, Sunny Sunshine perched atop her shoulder and a steaming mug of tea in each hand. "Hard day already?"

Summer groaned. "I just keep wishing that if I shut my eyes hard enough I could go back to yesterday."

Iris laughed in response. "If you figure that out, let me know how, too. We'd both be filthy rich!" She motioned for Summer to sit up. "Here, tea."

Summer accepted the warm mug of what turned out to be English Breakfast with plenty of milk and sugar. The mug had a smiling sun on its front, but Summer didn't want to smile today—not for that sun or anyone else.

"Drink up," her aunt urged. "It's good for the soul. Good for the heart too."

Summer turned the mug around so she didn't have to look at the smiling sun anymore. She sighed and asked, "If you could go back in time, Aunt Iris, where would you go?"

"I'd stay right here," Iris said without hesitation.

Summer thought about this for a moment. "But your whole life you saved up for that cruise, and now that it's over, don't you feel sad?"

"No, I'm happy that I got to go. I'll keep those memories with me forever."

"Are memories enough, though?" She frowned, but Aunt Iris continued to smile.

"Sometimes they have to be."

"Did you ever fall in love?"

"My, lots of questions today!" Iris chuckled. "Of course I've fallen in love. A bunch of times. It's impossible to go through life without finding it at least once."

"Then how come you ended up alone?" Oh, she hoped that hadn't come out rude.

Her aunt just winked at her, took another sip of tea, then said, "Who says this is the end, huh?"

"You know what I mean." Summer had her whole life laid out before her. Why couldn't she be happy like this? Maybe she had taken after her mother more than she'd thought.

Iris placed a hand on Summer's shoulder and gave it a squeeze. "Sometimes God gives us obstacles so we can prove to ourselves how much we really want the things we think desire."

"So leaving means I didn't want to be with Ben badly enough?"

"Oh, darling. It's not over until you're six feet under. Give it time. You'll get there."

Summer sighed. "I wish I was *there* already, wherever that is."

"Don't wish your life away. The best is yet to come." Summer was pretty sure she'd seen both of those sayings on one of her aunt's many coffee mugs, but decided not to point that out.

Iris held up an index finger and cocked her head to the side.

A moment later the doorbell gonged.

"I'm not ready to say good-bye," Summer whispered. She also hadn't made any effort to put herself together for the day, but that seemed less important now.

Iris shrugged. "Then don't." And with that, Iris breezed away, leaving Summer more confused than ever.

Chapter 25

Ben waited in the living room with Aunt Iris and Sunny Sunshine while Summer got dressed. "Did you have a good trip?" Ben said, doing his best to make small talk with a woman he hardly knew, though he'd been acquainted with her his whole life.

"You know it. In fact..." Iris grabbed her tablet from the coffee table, unlocked it, and handed it to Ben. "Pictures will make the waiting go by faster."

They scrolled through beach after beach punctuated with pictures taken all over an elegant cruise ship. Iris was no stranger to the selfie and seemed to have invested in a selfie stick for the trip. She'd clearly made lots of friends during her trip, mostly with other middle-aged and elderly ladies, but a certain gentleman kept popping up in several of the shots...

"A little summer romance?" Ben marveled at how easily talking with Iris had become in the span of a few short minutes. She was Summer's family, after all, and the reason his dream girl had turned up to Sweet Grove in the first place. That made her his own personal hero.

"You're one to talk," she teased. A smile spread across her face, and her eyes became unfocused as if looking into the past instead of the brightly decorated living room around them. "That's Monty. A fancy name for the most down-to-earth man I've ever known."

Ben wanted to ask more, but Summer stepped into the room and everything else in his world was immediately forgotten. She wore a bright yellow sundress and had her hair swept up into a bun. Not a speck of makeup showed on her face, and Ben liked it that way. He could even see the adorable freckles she tried so often to cover up.

He shot to his feet and pulled her into a hug.

"Kiss her!" Iris called, and Ben didn't hesitate to follow instructions.

"Well, good morning to you too," Summer answered.

"Are you ready to go?" Ben stole a quick look at his watch and realized that they were already a bit late for what he had planned.

"What's the rush?" Summer looked toward her aunt, who simply shrugged and passed Sunny Sunshine from one hand to the other.

"If this is my last day with you, then I'm not going to waste a single second." He kissed her again, then asked, "Remember that night when we jumped off the bridge at the Cider Mill?"

"Of course, I do. That's one of my favorite memories of us."

"Well, I thought we could head back one more time. Maybe throw a penny or two down the old wishing well while we're at it."

"Only if you promise me one of those delicious apple turnovers while we're there."

"Oh, Summer, I would never deprive you of that."

"Then let's go." She grabbed his hand and pulled him out the door. It seemed she didn't want to waste a single second either.

At the cider mill, they walked hand in hand down the path that led to the old bridge.

"I can't believe this is our last time here together," Summer whispered. As if saying it louder would somehow make it even truer.

Ben reminded himself not to be sad, that it wasn't over yet and if his plan worked, it wouldn't be over at all. He asked, "You'll come to visit your Aunt Iris sometimes, right?"

"Well, yeah, but probably not more than once a year." She kicked at a pebble as they continued to forge ahead.

Ben stopped walking and pulled her to his chest. "Then visit me, too." He only needed to keep his surprise for another five minutes or so, and to do that he had to act natural.

"*Ben,*" she warned.

"Yeah, I know, I know. Can't blame a guy for trying though, right?" He gave her what he hoped looked like a sad smile.

"Thank you." She pulled away from him to continue down the trail, but he held tight to her hand. He gave her another kiss before allowing her to continue toward the bridge.

"Ben?" she asked once they were walking again.

"Yeah?"

"Why did you choose to bring me to the bridge today?"

He shrugged. "Why not?"

"Is it because we both promised to not be afraid and took that leap of faith?"

"Maybe."

"And you think that by taking this job, I'm being afraid?"

"I didn't say that."

"But you do." Summer frowned, then bit her lower lip.

"Hey, those are your words, not mine."

"When promises run out, words are all we have left."

"Who's Confucius now?" he joked, recalling another memory from that night.

"Ben, I mean it. What else is there left to say other than good-bye?" Even though the day had only just begun, tears already threatened to tarnish her beautiful face. No, he couldn't keep this from her for another second. He couldn't let her cry, if there was any way to avoid it.

Ben pulled her back to him and kissed each of her eyelids in turn. "Summer, I'm not the only one who's going to miss you. I'm not the only one who needs to say his good-byes."

"What?" she sniffed.

"Look." He pointed into the distance. "You should be able to just see the bridge from here."

"Are those… balloons?"

"Maybe."

"Ben, what did you do?"

"I don't know," he answered with a smile. "Race you to find out?" He took off at a slow jog, reaching out for Summer's hand as he went. This time they reached the bridge together, hand in hand. The entire town of Sweet Grove—or, at least, just about—had crowded onto and around the bridge. A hand-painted banner hung from the railing they'd once jumped off. *Bon Voyage*, it read.

Balloons flanked the entry point of the bridge. Tables had been set up with food and drink and presents—all the proper fixings for a party. And in that moment, Ben thanked his lucky stars for a friend like Maisie. She'd arranged everything to his specifications and then some, giving him the chance to prepare the other part of the surprise for Summer.

"Surprise!" everyone shouted.

Summer brought both hands to her mouth in shock and delight. And she cried anyway, but Ben was pretty sure they were happy tears—and they hadn't even gotten to the best part yet. How he hoped she would like it!

He'd taken his mother's advice to heart. In order to be the best man for Summer, he also had to be the best man for himself. And this was his chance to reveal everything and hope she liked what he had to show for himself—to show for them.

Summer couldn't believe her eyes. While she'd always made friends easily, none of them had ever thrown her such a marvelous party—and a surprise at that.

"Do you like it?" Ben asked, gazing at her hopefully.

"I love it!" she shouted for everyone to hear, and then just for Ben, she whispered, "I love you." Sure, she had promised she wouldn't say it today, told herself it would only make saying good-bye that much harder, but he needed to know how much he mattered to her, that she'd stay if she could.

Their eyes locked, and she thought she saw the hint of mystery lurking in Ben's beautiful greens, but before she could figure out what he might be hiding, he gave her a quick peck and said, "I'll be right back, okay?"

"Ben, where are you—?"

Elise, Jennifer, and Kristina Rose ran up and surrounded her in a group hug.

"Are you surprised?" Jennifer squealed.

Summer nodded enthusiastically. *"Very."*

"The best is yet to come," Elise said, and the other two women immediately hushed her.

"Don't ruin it," Kristina Rose warned.

"What?" Elise argued. "She doesn't know what I mean. Look, there's Ben now anyway."

They all turned to where Ben stood in the center of the slightly curved bridge, which served as the perfect impromptu stage.

"Summer, will you come here?" He reached both hands toward her and waited for her to join him.

"What's this all about, Ben?" She still had no idea. Although she was starting to suspect that maybe...*No, no assumptions. Just enjoy it.*

"I want you to stand right here," he said, planting each of his feet firmly on the old bridge. "Each of us has something we want to tell you, okay?"

She nodded, expecting Ben to say more, but he simply stepped aside to reveal a line of townspeople who were each waiting for that chance to speak one on one with Summer.

Maisie was first. She had her arm looped through an older man's elbow. Summer hadn't seen him before, but he bore a strong resemblance to each of the Bryant men.

"Summer," Maisie said, "I'd like you to meet my dad, Mayor Matthew Bryant."

"Oh, hello." Although stunned, Summer remembered her manners and reached out to shake hands.

"Hello, young lady," the mayor said. "I understand you've made quite the impression on my town and all the people in it. Have you enjoyed your stay in Sweet Grove?"

"Yes, very much. You have a lovely community here," Summer answered.

Maisie grinned so big, it looked as if she were about to burst. "Tell her. Tell her now, Dad! I seriously can't wait another minute."

Mr. Bryant chuckled. "Hold your horses, Maisie. You always were in too much of a rush."

"What's going on?" Summer looked from one Bryant to the other, then searched the crowd for Ben, who was nowhere to be seen.

"As my over-exuberant daughter just told you, I'm the mayor of this here town. Have been for nearly thirty years now as a matter of fact. It's with great pride and joy I've watched it grow ever bigger and bigger. I'm afraid Maisie's little notice board at the grocery store just isn't enough to get the word out about important goings-on. As Maisie so astutely pointed out to me, I could accept a bit of official help with that."

"He wants to give you a job!" Maisie shouted, still shaking with glee.

Well, this was definitely not what she had expected. "A job?"

"The title is fancier than the actual role, but I'd like to hire you to start up the new Sweet Grove Sentinel, a proper town paper. Besides reporting on the events, you'd also get to help plan them. Keep bringing the town together as you already have been. Besides, I understand communications are a bit of a specialty for you?"

"Yes, I majored in communications."

"The high school could also use someone to pick up the drama club, what with Mrs. Green retiring come spring. Ben tells me you're phenomenal at, umm, *actressing* was it?"

Summer laughed. "If I do say so myself. Theater was my minor."

"It will be a lot of work, but I could sure use someone with your skills. Just tell me, are you comfortable with using a computer to do your reporting? We can print a paper on Sundays to give out at the church, and keep up with the news on a special Sweet Grove Sentinel blog during the week.

That's what all the modern small towns seem to be doing these days, and I want to make sure we can keep up."

"Dad, you can tell her all the details later. For now, I just want Summer to say she'll stay. Please, please stay in Sweet Grove," Maisie pleaded. "Daddy is a great boss. You'll like working for him. I do!"

It was all happening so fast. She liked the sound of everything, but she needed a moment to herself to process it all. Private moments, however, were in short supply, seeing as she was the guest of honor at this particular party.

"That's very nice, I..."

Before she could fully form an answer, Maisie and her father stepped aside and the next person in the receiving line stepped forward.

"Aunt Iris? You knew!"

"Of course I knew." Aunt Iris bobbed her head, and Sunny Sunshine, who was in a little birdy harness that resembled a tuxedo, bobbed right along with her. "And we want you to stay too, Summer. Stay and keep living with me and Sunny Sunshine. Just stay the heck out of Morning Glory's, would you? It will take me weeks to get my records in order again. I supposed I just won't have time to keep up with the gossip on top of that, and I'm so out of sorts after being away for the last couple months. Bout time I gave up gossip and let someone else do official reporting. Don't you think?"

"Oops, sorry about that." Summer blushed and accepted a hug from her aunt.

Next Jennifer, Elise, and Kristina Rose skipped forward.

"Sorry I almost ruined the surprise," Elise said. "I just get too excited sometimes. And I really, really want you to stay."

"Yeah, we could use someone with your... *spirit* as a regular for karaoke night," Kristina Rose said with a giggle.

"And we could use a new best friend too," Jennifer added. "Stay, okay? We all already love you so much!"

One by one each of the people Summer had met during the past couple months came up to tell her why she needed to remain in their town.

"You really have a way of bringing this town together," Jeffrey said. "First the great Sunny Sunshine escape and now this. News seems to follow you. Might as well take advantage of that. You're the perfect person to give this town an official news outlet, and you seem to be perfect for my boy Ben, too. Stay!"

Jeffrey stepped back into the crowd, and Summer thought she heard Aunt Iris say "Escape? What?" But by then the next person had come to make his case.

Jack Bryant grinned at her and said, "If you promise to stay, I'll make you fresh apple turn-overs whenever you want. I mean it. That's how bad we all want you to keep on being our neighbor."

Even Pastor Bernie and his wife Tabitha were there. "Sometimes God's plan is a little less than clear, but sometimes it's so dag-nab bright that it's like looking at the sun. God brought you here for a reason, Summer, and God wants you to stay for a reason, too."

At last, after everyone had taken a turn to make their case to Summer, Ben came forward once more. "You already know I want you to stay," he said. "So instead of telling you why I need you so much, I'm going to tell you what I plan to do in order to deserve you. Summer, you swept into this town and fixed my broken life, simply by being wonderful, lovable, *awesome* you.

"When Stephen died, I never thought I could find a way to be happy again, but these past couple months have been happier than any life I could have ever imagined for myself. You gave me the courage to finally get my mother the help she needed and she's thriving. You make me brave. You make me realize that I don't have to settle in life, that by having one dream, I can also have them all. Summer, I'm going to finally go to college.

"Don't worry, I'm not asking you to stay, just so that I can up and leave. But I'll be going to an online university. I'll tell you all the details later, but I've already applied, and my grades in high school were great, and I might be able to get a scholarship even. And it will just work out. I know that in my heart.

"What I'm trying to say is… Summer, you're not just my dream girl. You're the girl who has single-handedly made all of my dreams come true. I guess that's what love does to you. It makes everything better. You made everything better, and you haven't just touched my life or my mom's. Everyone in Sweet Grove loves you and wants you to stay. I want you to stay. Not just for another week or month or year. I can't picture even a single day without you at my side. Summer, I want you to stay forever. I want to be there for you forever.

"Please say you'll marry me." He took a deep breath and waited.

But Summer didn't make him wait for long. "Oh my gosh, yes!" she cried.

All of their guests cheered as Summer and Ben embraced and shared their first kiss as a newly engaged couple.

Elise and Jennifer wasted no time in pulling the bon voyage sign from the bridge. They flipped it over, waving it high in the sky above their heads. *Welcome home*, the sign now read.

"Welcome home," her fiancé said with so much love in his eyes she almost couldn't believe any of this was true.

And in that moment, Summer knew beyond the shadow of a doubt that she was right where she belonged, where she'd always belonged.

Home.

Epilogue

Kristina Rose eyed the sheet cake longingly. Normally she'd take a big corner piece with extra rosettes for herself, but not this time. Had food really become such a big part of her life that she couldn't even get through a single party without gorging herself?

"Eat to live, don't live to eat," her mother had always said, yet she did the same exact thing. In fact, she was the very person who'd introduced Kristina to her addiction at an early age. Kristina tore her gaze away from the treat table and watched the happy couple hug and kiss in the wake of their engagement.

Summer looked positively radiant in her A-line sundress and with her natural curls teased and highlighted from the sun with little streaks of blond.

She looked like a fairytale princess—or at least the twenty-first century version of one. Kristina Rose sucked in her stomach and tried to hold her breath in, but it was no use. Nobody wrote love stories about fat girls, especially not fat small-town waitresses with nothing going for them but their winning personalities.

That's what her family had said growing up. "You're such a sweet kid, such a pretty face. If only..." They never finished those sentences, but Kristina Rose knew exactly what they meant to say. If only she weren't so heavy. If only she took better care of herself. But despite her love for food, Kristina did take care of herself. She drank at least eight glasses of water per day, always managed to snag at least seven hours of sleep each night, took long walks on her lunch breaks, and went through nightly beauty routines to keep her skin and hair glowing. So why couldn't she just stop eating?

"You're trying to fill a void," said the psychologist she'd met with as part of her mandatory surgery prep. "Even with surgery, you'll never keep the weight off unless you can uncover the source of that anxiety that's driving you to eat."

That all made perfect sense, but begged more questions rather than giving even a single answer.

She'd wracked her brain trying to *uncover the source* as she'd been instructed, but ultimately had come up short. Now her surgery loomed just a couple weeks away. In two weeks, a big city doctor she'd met only a couple times before would slice her open and reroute her intestines, taking out a sizable chunk of her stomach in the process. Then she would have to learn a new way of eating, a new way of living. But she would get a new body out of it, a healthier one.

No more diabetes, no more plus-sized clothing. Or at least that's what they all hoped and felt reasonably certain would happen. There were, of course, exceptions to every rule, and Kristina had prayed long and hard that she would not be one of them.

Now her life was in the doctor's hands, quite literally. She would have to trust him and trust in God as she started the next chapter of her life's story. But who would she be if not that fat girl that was everyone's friend, but nobody's girlfriend?

Kristina Rose had never even been kissed, not once. Talk about pathetic for a twenty-something, but boys just hadn't been interested in her that way. And in seeing that, Kristina had done everything she could to shut off that need center in her heart.

Friends could be enough. Food could be enough. But now food could no longer be an option. Which left...

Her friend Jeffrey strode over to her with a flute of champagne clutched in each hand. "They're about to toast to Ben and Summer," he said. "I didn't want you to miss out."

"Thank you," Kristina said, accepting the glass and choosing not to point out that she would no longer be allowed to drink once the surgery had been performed. The doctor and psychologist both said her surgery would put her at a much higher risk of developing alcoholism, that so many people chose to substitute one addiction for another and that her tinier stomach wouldn't be able to handle nearly as much alcohol. It would zip right through her, make her loopy.

But for now, she would toast. She would drink. She would smile and wish the new couple luck.

She and Jeffrey clinked glasses and she had to bite back a laugh when the champagne's fizzy bubbles tickled her upper lip.

"Good stuff, isn't it?" Jeffrey asked, smacking his lips. "I've never been much of a drinker, but I could get used to this."

She nodded, smiled, did her Kristina Rose thing.

"I'm really happy for Ben and Summer," he continued. "Aren't you? I mean, it must be so nice knowing you've found the person you're going to spend the rest of your life with. Knowing you'll always have someone in your corner, no matter what." Jeffrey smiled at her and let his eyes fall to the lip of her glass which she held close to her chin.

"I can't even begin to imagine how nice that must feel," she admitted and took another long drink.

"Oh, you've finished. Can I top you off?" Jeffrey held out his hand and waited for the glass.

Kristina hadn't even realized she'd finished the champagne in two gulps. That was probably the reason she was so fat to begin with. Didn't even realize when she'd downed a bag of chips or half a gallon of ice cream. Maybe she was hiding something from herself after all.

"You don't mind?" She handed Jeffrey her glass, and their fingers brushed against one another's. She felt a small thrill run through her, but then realized it must be the champagne getting to her head already. She and Jeffrey had been friends for years. They even worked together at Mabel's on Maple for the past several years as well. He was one of her best friends, and—sure—she'd always found him handsome, but she'd also always brushed those feelings aside. After all, she wasn't the type of girl men waged wars for. She wasn't even the type of girl men threw parties for or sent bouquets of flowers to. She was Kristina Rose, plain and simple and oversized.

"Of course I don't mind." He watched her for a few beats, then ran off toward the refreshment table to refill both glasses.

She'd better watch it with Jeffrey, otherwise she'd find herself longing for two things she could never have.

The next installment in the First Street Church Series, LOVE'S PROMISE, is coming soon. Make sure you are signed up for Melissa's newsletter, so you don't miss out! You can do that at www.MelStorm.com/gift

***

If you enjoyed LOVE'S PRAYER, you'll also enjoy Melissa's books about angels, the Pearl Maker Series, which starts with DIVING FOR PEARLS.

Although Elizabeth died giving birth to her daughter, her death wasn't the end. She awakens to find her sacrifice has transformed her into a special kind of angel—a protector—and if she is able to help her charge through the Pearly Gates, she too will be welcomed into Heaven.

Elizabeth is both heartbroken and overjoyed when she finds she'll be watching over Daisy, the daughter she never got to meet. She'd like nothing more than to live with her little girl in paradise, but being a guardian is hard work. Will Elizabeth be reunited with her daughter, or forced to suffer in silence as she watches Daisy make mistakes that place her just out of Heaven's reach?

Now please enjoy this excerpt from DIVING FOR PEARLS.

The unyielding wall of white surrounded her like an embrace, absorbed her, became her. Nothing existed except for the vast blankness. She drifted through it, a mere ripple in the endless ocean. Time passed, but not in any discernible way. She didn't know where she was or why, but she also didn't think to question this new plane of existence. It, like she, just *was*.

The milky infinity at last separated to reveal the silhouette of an enormous city on the horizon. And this city was made of all the most spectacular colors in the sky's repertoire—pinks, purples, oranges, yellows, blue—an impossibly beautiful structure built of sunrise. Flanking the ethereal village stood two soaring gates made of the finest yellow gold and dotted with pearls, each of which loomed larger than the distant moon.

The current carried her forward, but before she could pass through the gates, a figure materialized to bar her entrance.

"Elizabeth," it said, and at once she remembered who she was and how she had come here.

I died—the acknowledgment flooded her awareness, but it did not make her sad. Her body now formed around her, but it felt clunky and foreign.

"I am Peter," the man said as his body also materialized before her—a dimpled chin, wavy blond hair, and long limbs. The perfect likeness of someone she knew very well. *Theo.*

"You look exactly like my husband, but how?"

"I made myself familiar to give you comfort, for we have much to discuss."

"Am I in Heaven?" she asked, already sure of the answer.

"Yes. Do you remember how you died?"

Elizabeth thought back to her last moments on Earth. A cry escaped before she could choke it back. "Please tell me, Peter—is my baby okay?"

"Yes, she is. Your sacrifice saved her."

Her? I had a girl? Tears of joy sprang to her eyes. As magnificent as her new home had proven, she also couldn't bear the thought of never knowing her daughter, of leaving her baby without a mother, leaving her husband without a partner.

Peter placed a hand on her shoulder, and although she couldn't feel it, the gesture still brought comfort. He waited until her racing thoughts slowed, waited for her to work her situation out, and continue their conversation.

"So is this it? Do I cross through those gates, and never see my family again?" She raised both arms to motion toward the gates—so tall they appeared to carry on forever into the sky.

"Your life is over, yes, but this is not the end of your journey. You are not ready for Heaven, Elizabeth."

Fear took hold as she murmured, "Are you sending me to that other place?"

Peter chortled. "No, no, not at all. But, you see, you aren't yet ready to cross through those gates and become a Pearl. Your heart is still tied to the world. To live here, your heart must be free and ready for paradise."

"I… I don't understand."

"You've proven your capacity for great love by sacrificing yourself in order to save your daughter. You also miss her and need her in the same way she will need your protection as she goes through life. While I cannot undo what has already been done, I can send you back to Earth. You will be transformed into a special kind of angel, a protector."

"You're making me a guardian angel?"

"Yes, so you can watch over your daughter and

know your sacrifice was not in vain, so you will complete your unfinished business, and so that you will be ready. Come with me. I will make everything clear."

***

And don't forget to sign up for Melissa's newsletter, so you can find out about each new book the moment it is released!

AFTERWORD

Why do we read, write, learn, live? For me, the answers are all one and the same. I write in order to explore deeper questions, in order to think and get others to think, in order to stretch the bounds of my imagination, in order to grow.

Life is a journey and it's one that each of us can only take for ourselves. Sure, others can travel alongside us, but no one can step into *your* shoes and do it for you. And an important part of life to me and to many others is spirituality, finding how we relate to the larger world, and figuring out why we're even here to begin with.

This brief afterword isn't about my personal beliefs, but it is about some dangerous assumptions people have made about me and other authors who choose to address moral and spiritual issues.

It is so, so important to address these beliefs outside of a traditional Christian Fiction model. For me, spirituality doesn't happen within the confines of a church, a temple, or mosque. It doesn't follow a specific course of rules and regulations, and faith is something we must exercise in all aspects of our lives, not just when dogma dictates or when it's convenient, or expected, or safe.

Sometimes life is hard. Sometimes it's ugly. But every new situation is a chance to grow in your faith and to grow in all the great things that make you *you*, and tie you both to God and to your fellow man/woman.

I believe in kindness despite any differences in beliefs, and I believe in sharing goodness with all people, not just those who believe the exact same things I do. I like to think, I like to be challenged, I like to grow in self-awareness and in my personal spirituality. That's why I write about the things I do. Heck, that's why I write. It's that constant, hungry pursuit of a higher wisdom, of becoming better than I am, of doing good.

I'm not a fan of preaching to choirs, nor preaching really, because I believe spirituality is deeply personal. I write for myself and for my daughter, for anyone who is interested in reading enjoyable stories that raise some important questions but ultimately allow you to answer those questions for yourself.

I want ALL people to be able to read and connect with my books (if they choose to) and to be able to contemplate the spiritual and moral issues raised—not just Jews, not just Muslims, not just Christians.

Just people.

And that's why I'm not a Christian Fiction author, though I choose to explore spirituality as a prominent theme in my writing and often write about Christian characters. If you'd like to further explore these themes with me, I urge you to check out my *Diving for Pearls* series and to keep an eye out for more First Street Church Romances.

Diving for Pearls started as a thought exercise following my near-death experience in birthing my daughter, but it quickly became a love letter to my little one, and evolved even further to encompass my answers to all of life's most difficult questions.

What is the meaning of life?

Why do bad things happen to good people?

Is Heaven real? What is it like? What about Hell?

Are angels among us?

This deeply personal story provides my answers, answers that have given me peace as I face each new obstacle in life, as I watch my baby grow into a young lady, as I continue to strive to live life to its fullest, and just to be—and it does it all through the journey of a mother-turned-guardian angel.

While I plan to write many more stories about my angels, I also have so much more in store for the small but lovable town of Sweet Grove, TX. This colorful cast of unforgettable characters will each have the chance to find pure and lasting love, thanks to their involvement in the small town church.

Well, that's enough about me and my projects!

How about *you?* What do you believe, and how do choose to explore it? I hope this story and others like it have brought you a little joy and that it's made you think, too.

Until next time, let's all read, write, learn, and live the best we can.

Love,

Melissa S.

ALSO BY MELISSA STORM

The Cupid's Bow Series

When I Fall in Love

My Heart Belongs Only to You

I'll Never Stop Loving You

You Make Me Feel So Young

Total Eclipse of the Heart

Tainted Love

I Want to Dance with Somebody

You Belong with Me

She Will Be Loved

Somebody Like You

All I Want for Christmas is You

The First Street Church Romances

Love's Prayer

Love's Promise

Love's Prophet

Love's Trial

Love's Treasure

Love's Testament

Love's Redemption

Love's Resurrection

Love's Revelation

The Book Cellar Mysteries

Walker Texas Wife

Texas & Tiaras

Remember the Stilettos

Ladies, We Have a Problem

The Pearl Makers

Angels in Our Lives

Diving for Pearls

Love Forever, Theo

Shackle My Soul

Angel of Mine

Stand-Alone Novels & Novellas

A Texas Kind of Love

A Cowboy Kind of Love

A Wedding Miracle

Finding Mr. Happily Ever After

A Colorful Life

My Love Will Find You

The Legend of My Love

Splinters of Her Heart

Melissa also writes Children's Books and Nonfiction as Emlyn Chand. Learn more about those works at www.EmlynChand.com.

ACKNOWLEDGMENTS

This is always the hardest part of the entire book—figuring out the thank yous!

First and foremost, I must always thank my wonderful husband, Falcon. He makes everything possible an in every way possible. From being an amazing stay-at-home dad for our little girl to taking care of me, the house, all the pets, and just always knowing how to encourage me to keep going. Also he kind of taught me the meaning of love in the first place, helped me to understand the constant battle of depression, and served as the final proofreader for *Love's Prayer* too!

Next up we have my Super Reader team, and especially Heidi, Rosemary, Rhonda, and Jasmine. Their enthusiasm for this story, this series, and my writing on the whole has also encouraged me to take my writing even more seriously and to make sure I get those word counts in each and every day. They are my readers, my friends, my tribe, and I appreciate them more than they may ever know.

My production team must also be thanked—and

praised! To my uber talented cover designer, Mallory Rock, to my exceedingly patient and ridiculous smart editor, Stevie Mikayne.

Then there are my author friends like Bella Andre, Barbara Freethy, Bonnie Paulson, K.M. Hodge, Melissa McClone, and so many others, who continue to believe in my work and get excited right along with me.

My family for giving me a spiritual upbringing and teach me about the Bible and about God. Our rabbi, Ariana Gordon, and all the amazing folks at Temple Israel who took us in with open arms.

Lastly, to Ducky, the real-life inspiration for Sunny Sunshine. Ducky was a close friend and beloved pet for eight years before he died unexpectedly right around the time I began writing this book. To help deal with my grief, I wrote some of my favorite memories of him into the story. Yes, the escaped parrot flying around the neighborhood and too afraid to land actually happened! Our neighbors brought seven ladders to help out. Rest assured, you'll be seeing more of Sunny Sunshine in Iris Smith's book titled *Love's Resurrection.*

And, of course, this is book is also to you—to you for taking a chance on this book and hopefully loving it.

Thank you. Thank you. Thank YOU!

About the Author

Melissa Storm is a mother first, and everything else second. She used to write under a pseudonym, but finally had the confidence to come out as herself to the world. Her fiction is highly personal and often based on true stories. Writing is Melissa's way of showing her daughter just how beautiful life can be, when you pay attention to the everyday wonders that surround us.

Melissa loves books so much, she married fellow author Falcon Storm. Between the two of them, there are always plenty of imaginative, awe-inspiring stories to share. Melissa and Falcon also run the business Novel Publicity together, where she works as publisher, marketer, editor, and all-around business mogul. When she's not reading, writing, or child-rearing, Melissa spends time relaxing at home in the company of her three dogs and five parrots. She never misses an episode of *The Bachelor* or her nightly lavender-infused soak in the tub. Ahh, the simple luxuries that make life worth living.

Learn more or connect with Melissa at
www.MelStorm.com

35300259R00152

Made in the USA
Middletown, DE
27 September 2016